All the best!

Denny Spencer

7-10

LISTENING
for the
BUGLES

A story about champions, tragedy, and triumph

DENNY SPENCER

Cover photograph taken by Denny Spencer
Featuring the eighteenth hole of Inverness Club, courtesy of Inverness

Special thanks to the Millcraft Paper Company; text printed on Millcraft 60# white offset; dustjacket printed on 80# gloss.

Book design by Erin Howarth, Wilderness Adventure Books
www.wildernessbooks.org

Illustrations by Cristina Mezuk, www.cristinamezuk.com

Manufactured in the United States of America

INTRODUCTION

The seed for this story started well over ten years ago, in the early 1990s. During that chapter in my life, I was traveling almost always alone, and usually by automobile. Nearly every week, I was faced with long drives to the next Senior PGA Tour event in my quest to qualify on Mondays for the following week's tournament. Fortunately, I played in several.

I had enjoyed a nice career as a competitive amateur golfer. But, as I approached my 50s, the fire still burned in my belly to find out just how far the game might take me. It was a gutsy move, but I decided to step off the virtual cliff and into the unpredictable. The next five years would become the hardest job I ever had, and without doubt, the greatest adventure of my life.

It was during those long periods of driving alone that the saga of Billy and JR Thompson began taking shape in the deeper recesses of my mind. For me, the story could have only been woven into the tapestry of my life's great passion, *golf.*

Most often, very small parts of the story would form in my thoughts, and rarely in any kind of order. But as the pieces grew, they seemed to attach themselves to relevant other pieces and became sections of the story. As those larger sections grew, they filled in the gaps and melted together to complete the overall sequence of events. The story simply evolved on its own.

As an example, I wrote the last chapter in the book almost at the beginning of this process. I always knew how the story would end and wanted, at least, to get those thoughts into my computer while others still lingered somewhere in the ether. I also knew, early on, the events that would impact the life of the story's main character, Billy Thompson. One of them would become the linchpin on which the rest of the story hinged.

Over the years, I came to know these people. They all became real in my mind. Many of the places, events, and people in *Listening for the Bugles* were inspired by places my golf career took me, a number of personal experiences (mostly special shots, caddy stories, and gallery reactions), and the many wonderful people I encountered. All of them befriended me along the way, and I will be eternally grateful.

I became convinced that there are very few coincidences in this life, that people are placed in your path to help you, to teach you, and to spur you on. None of us is complete. We all rely on others to shore up our weaknesses. I could never repay them for their unselfish generosity, their constant encouragement, and their own belief in chasing an improbable dream.

I would like to acknowledge a few of them for their love, their faith, and their support.

The first would have to be my dear mother, Thelma Spencer. No boy ever had a greater cheerleader than her. She encouraged and nurtured my dreams and told me often that dreaming produced "the songs in your heart," a line you will see woven into this story. Mother's long and rich life ended at age 91 in 2004. Hundreds of people paid their respects and all had stories of her wonderful sense of humor, her unselfishly total commitment to her family, and the love with which she showered her many friends. We miss her hearty laugh, but the imprints on the souls of my brother and me, and our families, are indelible.

I was also extremely fortunate to attract several faithful supporters who helped me financially and emotionally. They included my wife's parents, Al and Mary Marzano, and friends Jack and Suzie Bancer, Floyd and Pat Carey, Rick Elrod, Randy and Terri Faust, Greg Fish, Norm Kuhlman, Dick McIntyre, Don Michel, Pete Pilliod, Dean Roberts, Russ Senger, Jerry Sigler, Jim Smythe, and Tom Zraik. Thanks to you all for believing in me.

I will always be indebted to Pat Lindsay, former winner of the BC Open and 11-year PGA Tour veteran. It was Pat who first encouraged me to attempt a career on the Senior PGA Tour, one of the truly great compliments of my life. Upon my decision, Pat led me to Bloomingdale Golfers Club.

My friends Tim and Ruth Fennell, who became characters in this book, were so gracious in providing a place to stay in their home in Riverview, Florida during the five years I called Bloomingdale my winter home.

Dr. Jerry DeLeo, the first member I met, on the first day I arrived at Bloomingdale, became one of my closest friends and confidants during my professional career. Jerry taught me about metaphysics, which helped strengthen my mental approach to golf, a critical ingredient to success at that level.

Johnny Lavelle caddied for me during my last two years. He was intelligent, funny, well-read, and 100 percent in my corner. Everything was easier with him at my side. He and I became kindred spirits.

Jack O'Leary is a wonderful golf writer. He picked me out of the anonymity of Q-School and wrote some very flattering things. We've been friends ever since. He never fails to keep in touch to learn how my new career in golf course design is going.

Jack is a very good friend with whom to share a great cabernet.

Al and Kay Riegel became our life-long friends. Al, a fellow professional, and I traveled together a lot during the last few years of our Senior Tour odyssey. He and I traveled to Spain in 1996, and each of us gained membership on the European Seniors Tour that year. Al was also responsible for my entry into golf course design when my playing days ended. It's hard to imagine better friends.

Jennifer DeCamp, a book reviewer for the *St. Petersburg Times*, offered long hours of polishing my manuscript's first draft. I am grateful for her input.

My younger brother, Doug, is still one of the greatest natural athletes I have ever known. His special skills in football and baseball made everything look effortless, and he remains today, in his 60s, one of Inverness' finest golfers. Just watching him made me want to excel. I chose golf, one of my life's best decisions.

My son, Chip, who caddied for me in my first United States Senior Open in 1992 at Saucon Valley, Pennsylvania, has been a huge believer in my dreams and a constant source of inspiration and encouragement. My daughters, Amy and Jenni, have always shown a great deal of pride that their father actually *did* what he preached to them throughout their youth. "Follow your dreams. Stretch your talents as far as they will take you. *Never* be afraid to fail." They all took my advice. No man could be prouder of his children than I am.

I decided to save the best for last. On the day that Pat Lindsay first offered his belief that I was good enough to play on the Senior PGA Tour, I went home to share the news with my beautiful wife, Peggy. I asked her that night, "Honey, would you have a problem if I tried the Senior Tour when I turn 50?" Her immediate and unconditional answer was, "I'd have a problem if you *didn't.*"

From that day forward, she became totally involved with my next few years of planning and conditioning. During the five years I traveled, she stayed at home to continue her teaching career, with visits as a tour wife when I qualified for an event.

She encouraged me constantly, especially through the rough patches that come to every golfer. She reveled in seeing her husband, "inside the ropes," living his dream. I could always pick her sweet face out of a gallery. It was the one with the biggest smile.

Our marriage continues to be interesting, exciting, and full of mutual support. As we grow older, we occasionally reminisce about the many highlights of our life together. I always enjoy those moments. They are like verbally holding hands. They remind me that, without her, little of what I have accomplished would have actually happened, or meant nearly as much.

I hope you enjoy reading *Listening for the Bugles.* On the surface, it is a story about champions, tragedy and triumph, and it is *all* of that. But, just as with every round of golf, it is also a tale of how the direction of our lives is often influenced by the slightest of events, some of which we may not see coming, and how the quality of our awareness and preparation affects making the wisest mid-course corrections. In that respect, *Listening for the Bugles* is more a story about the journey of life itself.

There is a mystical and spiritual undertone to the story that I have often experienced myself. If you are lucky enough to be an avid golfer, there will be occasions when the game will reach inside and touch your soul.

That is what gives golf its lasting value.

—Denny Spencer

ONE

These paragraphs began my newspaper account of the United States Open Championship that concluded twenty-five years ago today.

TOLEDO, OHIO – **My deepest fear is that mere words will fail to chronicle what I have just witnessed. My heart rate is dangerously elevated, my brain is still swimming and my entire belief system has become totally suspended.**

Today, I stood at the edge of an epic battle, felt the thunder in my chest and heard the screams of thousands as a modern-day David stepped from the shadow of a new Goliath, loading his sling over and over, until the great giant fell. It was a struggle that transcended all of sport and one that history will surely judge the most astonishing final round in the annals of the United States Open Championship.

Nothing since, in any sport, has approached the drama or the exhilaration of that championship. So many personal reflections upon that battle, as well as my advancing age, have convinced me to finally relate all that fed the crescendo and ultimate climax of that magnificent day. After all, who better to tell the story than one who lived through and has been forever changed, by every phase of it.

I think you will agree. It just might rival the greatest golf story you will ever read.

My name is Mike Malloy.

My career as a sports writer began right out of college. For the better part of forty years, I covered just about every type of sporting event you could imagine. I found most of my assignments interesting, but after awhile, repetitious. That would all change on a warm August afternoon many years ago. That was the day I met Billy Thompson.

It's been a very long time since that meeting, even though in many respects, it seems like yesterday. I'm an old man now, and Billy…well, Billy's been gone for quite awhile. He was really a great guy, a true friend. After all these years, I still think about him almost every day. I really miss him.

Billy and I were about the same age and both of us were struggling to make something out of the careers we had chosen. Billy was driven to be a touring professional golfer. His choice was a lot tougher than mine. You might find that hard to believe. Golf looks so easy, so glamorous on television. But whenever *I* had a bad day at the office, if one of my articles was not up to snuff, I still made a living. Believe me, if you're not one of the few zillionaires at the top, the physical and emotional stress of professional golf, the constant travel, and the strain on family life can be enormous. I've witnessed it firsthand.

Billy was in town that day to play in a one-day customer outing for a large corporation. We met on the practice range before the event for an interview. Our bond formed almost instantly. We had a lot in common. Both of us were bachelors and although that made the crazy scheduling that our jobs demanded less complicated, each of us was getting tired of being alone. We loved red wine, baseball, and the occasional fly fishing or pheasant hunting trip. Our politics were pretty much in tune. And a well-written book, we agreed, could occasionally become your best friend on the road. He loved Notre Dame football; I was a rabid Ohio State fan. That night, we had dinner, a smooth merlot, and many laughs together. To my good fortune, we stayed in touch regularly from then on.

For a fellow like Billy who struggled to make enough money to stay in professional golf, those corporate outings were the unofficial paydays that often made the difference between red and black ink at year's end. He was, for the most part, a very solid player. His strength was putting. Occasionally, it went beyond phenomenal. He was simply magic with the flat stick. But, his weakness was his wildness with the driver. There were times when he could be downright pathetic.

Having been around professional athletes long enough to have formed some pretty strong opinions, I always felt Billy was one of the nicest and most genuine guys you'd ever want to meet, in or out of sports. To a man, my peers agreed with me. He was a lot of fun to be around and was sincerely interested in every person he met. It made him a natural, and in demand, for entertaining clients. With Billy, what you saw was pretty much what you got. He was the real deal. I loved the guy.

It breaks my heart when I think about what happened to him. That's part of the story I'd like to tell you. The other part, and certainly the most uplifting part, is how his son, JR, validated the one thing that Billy dreamed about ever since childhood.

Tonight, I'm here with JR at the Inverness Club in Toledo, Ohio to join their celebration of more than a century of involvement in American championship golf. Inverness has hosted a U.S. Amateur Championship, one U.S. Senior Open, two PGA Championships and five U.S. Opens. The last of those Opens finished here, twenty-five years ago today. That was JR's first U.S. Open, and his reason for returning this evening.

Just like every other time he's been back, he and I have walked together down to the eighteenth green behind the club's stately clubhouse. It's done with little fanfare, just the two of us, always with a minimum of conversation.

Being here helps us remember. Tonight is no different.

"Every time I come back to Inverness," JR is softly saying, "I love walking down into this narrow, green valley, especially late in the day with the shadows lengthening like they are now. Everything is so familiar, so vivid in my memory."

The peaceful silence of *this* particular evening contrasts greatly with the thunderous roars of past championship galleries who gathered around this outdoor cathedral, and especially the one that assembled here on that last day to watch JR finish. There would be several more Opens in JR's brilliant career, but none more memorable, or more stunning.

"Although it has been several years since we last came down here," JR adds, "it looks, and feels, and smells the same as the first day I laid eyes on this beautiful place. Remembering all that happened to me here, Uncle Mike, after all this time, it still doesn't seem quite real."

On the northern ridge sits the comfortable clubhouse of Inverness. Its view across the valley looks over the small and treacherous eighteenth green and the tree-lined ridge beyond. More than a century ago, the great golf course architect,

Donald Ross, came here to craft one of his many masterpieces. Because the valley and the course's finishing hole run from east to west, directly into the blinding late-day sun, modern designers might well have passed up such an opportunity. But Ross accepted what the ground provided and could not resist this natural setting to test each golfer with this deceptively difficult final par-4. All of golf can thank providence that he did. At only 354 yards, and growing increasingly short by modern standards, this devilish little hole has dashed many a contender's dreams.

"As you know, Uncle Mike," JR confides, "I've always been a little shy about public speaking. But, Inverness holds such a special place in my heart. I could never say no to whatever they wished of me. It should be fun to reminisce about that amazing day. But, if you don't mind, I'd like to spend a few more minutes down here to enjoy the quiet and breathe in a bit more of this special air before we go inside."

There's no hurry tonight, I'm thinking, but like I said earlier, I believe the time has come. After so many years, it's time to share with you what really happened here that day...how, and especially, *why* it all came to pass.

It is a story about champions, tragedy, and triumph...and so much more. Settle in and hang on. You're in for an interesting ride.

TWO

Good fortune, or maybe fate, had a great deal to do with Billy Thompson even becoming a golfer. He was raised, along with his younger brother, Jack, in a modest midwestern home rented by hard-working parents who were products of the Great Depression and World War II. Their goals were simple, to someday own their own home and give their two sons a life better than they had known.

Billy's father was a serious, practical, and private man whose standards of right and wrong had quite sharp edges. Any dreams he had harbored as a youngster about his own medical career were completely dashed by the Depression. He was a good man who loved his wife and sons, but he had a difficult time showing them the affection he felt in his heart. In his world, it seemed, strong men did not do such things. His own father, by example, had taught him well. He took responsibility seriously and none more so than his obligation to care for his little family. Work, to him, had become as natural as breathing.

Billy's mother, on the other hand, provided the emotional balance in their partnership. More than anything, she loved her boys unconditionally, showering them with affection at every opportunity. The home she created was a peaceful, happy one—clean and neat, with an aroma of something wonderful always wafting from her kitchen. She would see to it that her boys were well fed and clothed, something that she, orphaned at age five, did not always have.

Her home would also be a safe place for them to grow and learn. Her ease at story telling was legendary throughout the neighborhood and her hearty laugh was a product of a long line of theatrical people. However, her greatest gift, as Billy would often recall, was her constant encouragement that they follow their dreams, a positive and necessary first step to creating a successful, fulfilled life. Over and over, she encouraged them. "Never give up on your dreams, they are the songs in your heart."

Aided by his mother's constant encouragement, Billy fell asleep every night dreaming of becoming a great golfer and eventually becoming the U.S. Open champion.

Of the two boys, Billy's brother, Jack, was the naturally gifted athlete. His speed and instincts made every movement seem effortless. Rather than resent his brother, Billy admired him and vowed to someday be as good at *one thing* as his brother was at everything else. He knew it would take effort and would not come easy.

Luckily, that "one thing" happened early in his life, around the age of eight. A chance game of golf with borrowed clubs at a nearby municipal golf course was all it took. At first blush, he was hooked. There was nothing quite like the exhilaration of sweet contact, soaring shots, and imaginary applause. His life's first watershed event came at a tender age and convinced him. He would be a golfer.

Billy's passion for golf grew exponentially. It flowed through his veins and filled his heart. When the weather permitted, he could be found alone every day, after school, in a secluded little meadow at a nearby city park hitting golf balls. One of America's oldest municipal golf courses east of the Mississippi was only a short walk away. It afforded all the creeks and unmown areas necessary for an eager boy with a good eye to scout for balls given up for lost. Soon, his mesh potato sack was filled with a variety of worn and forsaken orbs that no real golfer would give second notice. But to Billy, they each became old friends who greeted him every day and offered their remaining life to his learning the game.

The meadow was surrounded on three sides with tall trees, and at the open end, a softball diamond. It offered lush turf and a multitude of targets. It was nearly always deserted, and save for softball season, quiet. It was the perfect place to work on his swing, to invent new shots, and more importantly, to conjure up real tournament visions and the thrilling roars of large galleries. Billy's imagination allowed him to play championship golf from the beginning and to feel the exhilaration of each successful shot. The fantasies were as real as the small boy's fertile mind could make them.

An elderly neighbor, upon hearing Billy's golf chatter, offered one of his life's greatest gifts, *Power Golf*, written by the great Ben Hogan and arguably, the most comprehensive golf instruction book of its era. By that time, Hogan had solidified his position as one of golf's immortals. He was also known, and greatly admired, for his miraculous comeback after a horrible accident in early February of 1949. It was an accident that should have killed the then reigning United States Open champion and his wife, Valerie.

Returning by automobile after a successful multi-week swing on the professional circuit, he and his wife were having a pleasant chat when, out of a bank of ground fog, swerved a Greyhound bus. Just before the head-on impact, Hogan instinctively flung himself across the front seat to shield Valerie. Although severely injured, it saved his life. The impact drove the steering column completely through the driver's seat.

His multitude of injuries included a double fracture of the pelvis and a broken collarbone. He lay flat on his back for forty-eight days, and although his survival was not in question, sadly, no one believed that Ben Hogan would ever play golf again. But Hogan's determination was of tempered steel. His life and golf were interchangeable. In only seventeen months following the accident, he hobbled to his second U.S. Open championship at Merion, confounding the experts. In 1951, he added his first Masters title, and a few months later, at Oakland Hills in Detroit, his third U.S. Open.

Following an off year in '52 when pundits began declaring the Age of Hogan to be over, he dumbfounded all of sport with wins at the 1953 Masters, the U.S. Open, and in the only attempt of his career, he added the British Open championship as well.

Prior to that British Open, Hogan spent a number of days walking the course at Carnoustie *backwards,* from green to tee. He did it each evening, after dinner, in what the Scots refer to as the gloaming. The late day shadows allowed him to pick out every hump and roll of the green surfaces and fairway approaches. Ben charted each feature and walked off meticulous yardages. His preparation was calculating and flawless, and led to the Scots referring to him as "the wee ice mon."

Hogan's dedication to detail and his never-ending search for perfection all shined brightly in his magnificent book. Billy's copy of *Power Golf* became dog-eared and frayed at the edges. Handwritten notes littered the margins. Many nights after lights-out, he would read beneath his blankets, flashlight in hand, until his eyelids turned to lead. Each new day brought him back to his private meadow, anxious to try the latest nugget gleaned from Hogan's book. In time, what Billy did not pour into golf, he simply did not have to give.

As the years passed, Billy's game outgrew the tiny meadow. The divot holes filled in, the target trees returned to being just trees again and the roars of imaginary galleries drew silent. But it was there that the seed was planted. A little boy with big dreams, sawed off clubs, and a precious book. Billy Thompson did indeed become a golfer.

THREE

Nearly every person who met Billy immediately liked him. He was a reasonably handsome and athletic young man with a slow, soft smile. Strangers were quickly comfortable and at ease. They saw a gifted golfer who generously shared his time and talent with fans, sponsors, and charities. He paid particular attention to kids, always trying to make them feel special. Although he was always amused that anyone would consider him a *hero,* he thought it was important to play that role for star-struck youngsters. His autographs to them uniformly began with the advice, *"Always do your best."* In some ways, he was still a kid himself and they loved him.

He was also a surprise hit with pro-am partners who, while writing large checks for the privilege of playing with a touring pro, had hoped to draw a "big name" player. But they quickly overcame their disappointment in a few short hours of his humor and personal attention during the day. Pro-ams with Billy were guaranteed...always fun.

However, as a child, and later as a grown man, he quietly dealt with a silent demon. One his father introduced him to.

Frank Thompson was a hard-edged product of tough times, a man who saw things only in black and white, no gray. He found little usefulness in a boy who would rather play games than work. In his world, dreaming at any age was a waste of time and it was often a source of disagreement with Billy's mother.

One night, through the paper-thin walls that separated their bedrooms, Billy heard his father's heated words and his mother's spirited defense of her firstborn.

"Jack's the one who'll make something of himself," he heard his father declare. "He's a *worker.* Billy is nothing more than a dreamer and I'm afraid all he'll end up with are broken dreams. I really don't think he'll amount to much."

The words stabbed him through the dark, making a gash on his soul that would never quite heal. He would often hear those words, over and over in his head, especially when things were not going particularly well.

Growing up, he developed a mindset to prove his father wrong. 'Someday,' he would often think, 'he'll brag to his friends that his son is the U.S. Open champion. *Then* he'll know...he'll know that he was wrong about me.' But the emotional pain became as bone-on-bone, always present, lived with and accepted as a part of his daily existence.

Billy and his father were wired as differently as day and night. Even as a young boy, Billy realized he would have to choose between pleasing his father and following his dreams. It was a sad choice. He knew instinctively that either direction would leave a large hole in his life. He would be right. Often, during his early years, he would excitedly run home to share stories of his latest round, or a new shot learned, only to be met with disapproval. After a while, only his mother would hear those stories and share his excitement.

Many a night, he would softly cry in his darkened room, wishing that someday his father would simply accept him. More than anything, Billy longed to hear him say, "I love you, son," or "I'm proud of you." Unfortunately, Billy's father died far too young. Those words would never come. His father's rejection would silently gnaw at him for all his days.

Billy would spend his life secretly craving acceptance and validation. For many people, such a circumstance can be debilitating. For Billy, it fueled his determination. The sadness in his heart helped produce the dreams. Golf would make them real.

FOUR

When Billy and I first met, he was not yet a regular face on the PGA Tour, having failed so many times at the annual nightmare of the tour's qualifying tournament, better known as "Q-school." For several years, he had knocked around various mini-tours throughout the country, working hard on his game to stave off the loneliness and to scrape together enough money to get to the next week's event.

Occasionally, he would qualify on Monday for that particular week's tournament on the PGA Tour. We would most often meet those weeks. I was, by then, regularly covering pro golf. Every time we got together, we would bring each other up to speed, share a good red, laugh, and tell stories. I often told him if he ever became famous, he was going to be the Tour's best interview. I can't remember a time, though, when he didn't need my reassurance that he would actually make it someday. I would always hesitate, and then say, *"Nah...not a chance!"* and we'd both laugh like hell. He knew I wanted it for him almost as badly as he did.

One of those meetings, however, really stands out in my memory. The story he told me *that* night was not about the usual light-hearted goings on of tournament golf, or some of the funny one-liners that the game produces. This one was more serious.

Billy and I were at dinner that night in Orlando. He had just finished a mini-tour event in Newburgh, North Carolina the week before. He knew that I loved his stories from the tour, and that I was especially fond of hearing about the characters he met along the way. Pro golf has a way of attracting an inordinate number of unique people. This story was about a unique person, to be sure, a new friend with a great deal of value.

Some tournaments in minor league golf staged pro-am events, others did not. It depended on how much support that week's particular venue could drum up, mainly from their local business community. In Newburgh, the pro-am prior to the tournament was fairly small, only ten or twelve foursomes. Naturally, Billy was one of the headliners, having charmed so many people there the year before.

In his group on that day was a large, robust man in his early fifties, Ralph Howe, the president of the local bank and head of Newburgh's Chamber of Commerce. He was a rather loud man, boastful even. He obviously enjoyed his status as a local celebrity.

Billy's job in pro-am events often involved catering to egos. Doing so would ultimately benefit the tour. He did it beautifully without sacrificing his own integrity. For Billy, it was simple. Get the man talking about himself and his success, tell a few foolproof jokes, then offer a tried and true golf tip or two. It was an effortless formula.

But the story he told me that night was not about Ralph Howe or the many others like him who Billy had met along the way. The story was about Howe's caddy that day, a middle-aged black man by the name of Spider Monroe.

Spider was a proud and humble man, immaculate in his dress and person. His trousers, somewhat frayed at the cuffs, were nonetheless creased as if ironed only minutes before. His white cotton shirt gleamed in the afternoon sun, accented with a real, hand-tied, black bow tie. He wore a light-colored tam to keep the sun off his balding scalp. Everything about him, especially the manner in which he carried himself, was military sharp.

Billy immediately noticed a gentle kindness that shown through his gaze and wide smile. Spider's skin was coal black, accenting his eyes and teeth. Upon introduction, their handshakes conveyed warm but powerful personalities. They liked each other at first glance.

Throughout the pro-am round, Spider attended to Howe's every need. But as they walked between shots, or waited for the group ahead to finish, Spider and Billy found a few moments to chat about a number of subjects, especially golf and baseball. Although Billy made sure every player in his group had a wonderful time, it was Spider Monroe who made that day's round interesting for him.

Following the pro-am dinner, Billy decided to do a little extra work on his driver and went to the practice range before beginning the 15-mile drive back to the hotel in town. He loved these late-day sessions. With sundown close at hand and everyone else gone, he could get the most from such practice.

"Evenin' Mr. Billy," came a familiar voice, breaking the silence.

Billy turned to see his new friend. "Hey, Spider, how you doin'? Thought you left after the round today."

"Well sir, I thought I'd stick around and see if you'd do me the favor of a ride back to the hotel. I live near there. You see, the way I figured it, it would be a whole lot quicker if I waited for you than if I had started walkin' right then." Spider's toothy smile was irresistible.

"Absolutely. I'd love the company." Billy chuckled. He was

15

thrilled for the chance to know more about this interesting man. "Just a few more balls and we'll be ready to go."

"Thank you, sir. I'd surely appreciate it," came the friendly response. Spider was now wiping each club with a fresh towel.

As they turned to leave, Spider hoisted Billy's large tour bag onto his broad shoulders. "It's the least I can do for a player of your caliber, Mr. Billy. Yes sir, I surely enjoyed watchin' you play golf today. I knew the minute I met you that you were a real professional, and that's the truth."

Billy knew the flattery was genuine. For a struggling pro in the minors, hearing it was not an everyday occurrence. It always felt good, especially from those who knew the game.

By the time they left, dusk had faded to nearly night and a light fog was beginning its inland roll from the nearby Atlantic. Their friendly chatter continued unabated as the truck's headlights carved their way through a number of foggy curves to Newburgh's downtown.

Billy looked at Spider, eyebrows raised in proposition. "How about a few beers before we call it a night, Spider? I'm buyin'. Meet you in the hotel bar in thirty minutes, OK?"

"Oh, I'd like that. Yes sir, I would. But, would you mind if I drank *red wine?*"

Billy's head turned to him again. "I *knew* there was something I liked about you, Spider," Billy replied with a grin. "How 'bout I pick out a nice cabernet?"

"Can't think of anythin' better, Mr. Billy, the wine or the company. Half an hour. I'll be there," Spider said, offering another firm handshake.

They settled in at a small table in a quiet corner of the lounge. Billy noticed that Spider had quickly showered and changed clothes. He liked that. It was another statement of personal pride. Spider's smile seemed even brighter without his hat.

"Franciscan cabernet is one of my favorites, Spider. I hope you'll enjoy it."

Spider's eyes widened. "I'm sure I will. Yes sir, I'm *sure* I will," as Billy poured a few ounces into Spider's wide-bowled glass. Spider lifted it to his lips and Billy waited for his reaction. He always loved sharing his favorites with another wine drinker.

"Mmm," came the reply. "'Bout as smooth as your back-

17

swing, Mr. Billy. Yes, sir. Thank you." His grin seemed a mile wide.

"Tell me, Spider, how'd you end up in Newburgh?"

"Well, sir, I actually *started* in Newburgh. When I was growin' up, my folks were sharecroppers nearby. Baseball took me away for some time, but I came back home several years ago. I've sort of come full circle. My job now with Mr. Howe is a good one. I caddy for him about three times a week and run errands and do odd jobs for him the rest of the time. He treats me real good, that's for sure. Baseball was my game then 'cause it didn't take much for poor people to play, just an open field, a bat, and a ball. I fell in love with baseball, real early in my life. I still remember the day the bug bit me."

Billy lifted his glass, "I'm all ears, my friend."

"Well, sir, it was one hot July day," Spider recalled. "I was about, oh, seven or eight at the time. A ball club done come to town for an exhibition. They were called the Kansas City Monarchs, one of the best teams in the Negro league at that time. Their best player was one of the greatest pitchers of all time, a fellow by the name of Paige. You ever heard of him?"

"*Satchel* Paige?" asked Billy. "Of course, what baseball fan hasn't heard of *him?*"

Spider nodded his head, pleased that his friend knew baseball. He continued, "He was a tall, lanky black man with so many speeds and deliveries, even the catchers couldn't keep track. His two best pitches, besides his blazing fastball, were known as the *hesitation pitch* and the *ghost ball.*"

Spider leaned to the right with his arm extended. "The hesitation pitch came from a sidearm style that almost stopped in mid-delivery. A lot of players thought it was a balk, but the umpires never called it. It really messed with a batter's timin'."

"And the ghost ball, oh Lordy, it was a pitch that had hitters shakin' their heads. They all said they could *feel* it go by. They even said they could *hear* it go by. But none of them ever said they could *see* it go by. Whenever old Satchel needed a strikeout bad, everybody knew the next pitch was gonna be one or the other.

"I'll tell you, Mr. Billy, everybody in town was so excited to see Satchel pitch, even the white folks. Seems like all of Newburgh was closed that afternoon.

"All us colored folks had to sit way out in the outfield bleachers, so when a ruckus started near home plate just before the game started, it took us awhile to figure out what was goin' on. Word spread like wildfire. You see, at that time, the New York Yankees had a rookie by the name of DiMaggio. You ever heard of *him?*" Spider queried with his head tilted sideways.

"*Joe DiMaggio?*" Billy asked with furrowed brow.

"Yeah, that's the one. Joe DiMaggio. You know, he became a pretty good player for the Yankees later on, but on that day, the Yankees wanted to test young Joe's batting skills to see if he had major league talent. I guess they figured the best test of all was to throw Joe up against old Satchel."

Spider was now leaning in closer to Billy, looking side to side as if someone else might be listening. "I'll tell you somethin', Mr. Billy, Satchel was not happy. He figured if the white men runnin' the major leagues wouldn't let him play because of the color of his skin, why should he allow one of *theirs* to come into his arena. We all kinda felt that way too, you see. It was natural."

"Of course," nodded Billy. "Perfectly natural."

Spider's blood was coming up a bit as he continued the story. "Finally, Satchel walked slowly to the top of mound and leaned in for the catcher's sign. Joe settled into the batter's box, movin' his bat back and forth. You could tell, even from right field, Joe was an athlete. Satchel shook off the first sign, then the second. Finally he was ready. He served up the first *ghost ball* that Joe would ever experience. It caused such a pop in the catcher's glove it even made us wince. Joe's bat never left his shoulder. I don't believe he ever saw that ball. The umpire raised his fist...*strike one.*"

Spider was mimicking the umpire's move with his fist in the air.

"Satchel caught the returning ball, turned his back to the plate, and kicked a little dirt toward the outfield. You could tell he was still boilin'. Then he turned and leaned in for another sign. He started shakin' off signs faster than the catcher could change 'em. Finally, he nodded. Into his windup he went. Halfway through his forward motion, everything seemed to stop momentarily. The crowd held its breath. It was the *hesitation pitch.* Joe had never seen anything like this one either. The ball looked like it was coming from somewhere near third base and it had flames comin' from it. Again, the bat never moved. *Strrrike Two,* came the call heard throughout the ballpark."

Spider was becoming quite animated now.

"Young Joe stood there, patiently, at the plate. Satchel was makin' him wait again. He shook off the first sign, then the second. All of a sudden, it dawned on nearly every one of us in the bleachers; look out now, Joe, here comes the *heat.* Sure enough, Satchel put a little extra rotation into his windup and released a rocket toward home plate."

"What happened then?" Billy wanted to know.

"Well, sir, in pure self defense, Joe just sorta stuck out his bat and hit a wounded flare out to short right field. The crowd gasped. Satchel slammed his glove to the turf, as Joe trotted down to first.

"Finally, Satchel loudly called *time out*. You could hear a pin drop throughout that stadium, everybody wonderin' what Satchel would do next. Finally, he snatched up his glove and walked toward young Joe standing on first base. About halfway there, he pointed his finger and in a loud voice full of prediction, he proclaimed, 'Let me tell you somethin', Mr. Joe. You might as well *sit down* right there on that bag, 'cause you ain't goin' *no place.*'

"Satchel returned to the mound poundin' his fist in his glove and in only *nine straight pitches,* he proceeded to strike out the side. With that final strike, Satchel looked over at Joe as much to say, 'Now get on outta here, boy.'"

Billy was smiling now. "What a great story, Spider. So that was the moment you got hooked on baseball, huh?"

"Yes, sir. Yes it was." Spider was now sliding back in his seat to relax. "I knew right then that I wanted to be a ballplayer."

Billy was fascinated. "So you ended up in pro ball?"

"Yes, sir. Yes I did," came the reply. His eyes reflected memories of his favorite years of life.

"How'd that happen?" Billy wanted to know.

"Well, sir, when I got old enough, about seventeen or so, I started workin' for the railroad, repairing tracks. I was real strong then, so liftin' steel rails, wooden ties and swingin' hammers was never a problem. I liked workin' too. The money was good and it helped me build an ever stronger body for baseball." Spider added modestly, "I hope you don't find me too boastful, Mr. Billy, but I could hit a baseball hard back then, *real hard.*"

"I'll bet you could," Billy said without doubt.

"Early that spring, a shiny silver train pulled into the station for about an hour's layover. An older man stepped out, followed by about twenty-five younger men, all white, except for two young black fellows. They were all clean cut and very athletic." Spider continued. "I went over to the older man and asked him what this group was. My clothes were tattered and dirty from workin', but he seemed to look past that. He told me that they had just finished spring training, and were headed back to California to start the major league season.

"'*Baseball?*' I asked.

"'Yes,' came his reply."

Spider was getting excited just re-telling the story.

"Now, I was just a naive North Carolina country boy with no one to guide me. So I blurted out, 'Sir, my name is Spider Monroe and I'm a great second-baseman. Can I go to California with you fellas?'

"The older man smiled at me and said, 'Well, it's nice to meet you, Spider. You look like a ball player. You're put together like a racehorse, son. But spring training is over for this year and our roster is set. How 'bout coming out to Anaheim next year for a try-out. That's near Los Angeles.'

"I was sure he was serious, because he gave me his business card and patted me on the shoulder." Spider reached for his back pocket. "I still have his card in my wallet. It's one of my most prized possessions."

Carefully, Spider slid the fraying card from deep inside his worn leather wallet. He gently handed it to Billy with immense pride. Billy held it closer to the table lamp. The ink had faded some, but he could still clearly read, *Bill Rigney, Manager, Los Angeles Angels Baseball Club*. Billy knew, as he looked up over the card to Spider's smiling face, that he was holding a treasure.

Spider carefully replaced the card and continued.

"I started savin' my money that very day. The first thing I needed for the try-out would be a new ball glove. It took a few months, but I finally was able to save enough to go down to Hansons Sporting Goods and buy me a new Wilson 2000, the best infield glove you could buy at the time. New gloves are always stiff, so I also bought some neatsfoot oil to help mold it to my hand. Every night, I'd oil it up and put an old baseball in the pocket. Then I'd tie it real tight with an old belt I had. After a time, it became part of me.

"A few more months of saving got me a new pair of Rawlings baseball shoes. They were made from the lightest leather known, kangaroo. I bought the red pair because they even *looked* fast."

"All winter, I dreamed of playin' baseball for a living. Even though I was a poor sharecropper's son who'd never been anywhere, I was never happier than those dreams made me." A small tear was forming in the corner of Spider's eye.

Billy had been silent throughout most of the story to this point. Suddenly it dawned on him. As contrasting as their backgrounds had been, coming from two completely different places, he realized how similar they actually were. Both of them were dreamers. Before he heard the rest of Spider's story, he knew the man in front of him had also heard the songs in his own heart. Could this have been the force that drew them together earlier in the day? He couldn't wait to hear more.

Spider paused and then continued.

"Come springtime, I hopped aboard a westbound freight train. For hours on end, I'd pound that glove's pocket with a ball. From the open door on that boxcar I'd watch the countryside pass by, all the while wonderin' 'bout what laid in store for me. All I had with me was a change of clothes, my new ball glove and them kangaroo shoes, all wrapped up and hangin' from a stick I rested on my shoulder. My momma had packed a couple of sandwiches and gave me a big kiss on the cheek when I left. Neither of us knew how long I would be gone or how far away the winds of my dreams would take me. But, she loved the fact that I was strikin' out on my own to follow my dream. She always encouraged us to do that."

Spider was slowly shaking his head, remembering the wonder of that moment.

"I still remember her face that morning, her big smile and tears streamin' down her cheeks. I knew they were tears of joy. I knew she was full of hope that I'd find a better life. I never saw her look so pretty as she did that day. It's still my favorite memory of her."

Spider lifted his glass again, mostly because his emotions needed a pause. A few more pleasureful sips before a welcome refill and he was back on course.

"It took the better part of five days, and more than a few trains, to finally get to California. Oh my, Mr. Billy, that's a *long* way from home. I was hungry, dirty and sore, but my spirit was never higher."

"When I asked for directions to the ballpark, I got some funny looks. I guess them folks never saw nobody from North Carolina before," Spider winked. "Did you know they got *two* ball clubs out there?"

Billy nodded, and Spider went on.

"Mr. Billy, that Anaheim Stadium was brand new, shiny as a new penny. The ball club was already on the field that morning, practicing for their opening day only a week away, against the San Francisco Giants. I could see Mr. Rigney from the top steps. He was standing next to the battin' cage. I couldn't wait to tell him I was finally there.

"After trotting down a long flight of stairs, I asked somewhat out of breath, 'Mr. Rigney?'

"He turned and said, 'What can I do for you, son?'

"'Well, sir, Mr. Rigney, I'm Spider Monroe from North Carolina. If you recall, last spring you told me to come see you 'bout a tryout? Well, sir, here I am.'

"He curiously looked me up one side and down the other. Then, remembering, he said, 'Well, I'll be damned.' He was scratchin' his head, and smiling. 'You came all this way?'

"'Yes, sir. Yes I did. For the tryout. Remember?'

"Mr. Rigney took a second or so to reflect, and then nodded his head.

"'Tell you what, Spider, you go on down to the equipment manager. Tell him I sent you. He'll show you where you can clean up a bit. Have him give you an Angels jersey and then come back out here, OK?'

"The other players were lookin' at me, all tattered and worn from my trip. Some of them were laughin'. But when they got a glimpse of that Wilson 2000 and them red kangaroo beauties, they weren't laughin' near as much.

"When I returned, Mr. Rigney asked me to step inside the battin' cage.

"'Let's see what you've got, son,' he said.

"I don't mind tellin' you, Mr. Billy, I was nervous. I missed the first couple of pitches I swung at, causin' those boys to start laughin' at me again. But then I settled down and found my stride. The first ball I hit was a line drive off the center field fence. The next three or four I got *real* solid, all long home runs to left."

"Finally Mr. Rigney asked, smilin', 'You always hit the ball that hard, Spider?'

"I said, 'Well, sir, actually I usually hit 'em a bit *harder*, but I haven't had nothin' to eat in three days. And to be honest, sir, I'm still a little stiff from that train ride.'

"Mr. Rigney raised his eyebrows and smiled at me again. 'Can you hit a few to *right* field for me?' he asked. And I did. Real long ones.

"'How 'bout some to center field, Spider?' So, I got hold of a couple more, directly over the 440 sign.

"I was waitin' for the next pitch when Mr. Rigney said, 'That's enough, son. There's somebody here who'd like to meet you.'

"I turned and another man had joined Mr. Rigney at the back of the cage. It was that singin' cowboy fellow who owned the club, Mr. Autry. Ever heard of *him?*"

"*Gene Autry* of the California Angels?" Billy asked.

"Yeah, that's him. They changed the name of the club that very year to go with the new ballpark. Mr. Rigney introduced me to him."

"What happened then?" Billy was dying to know.

"Well, sir, Mr. Autry was a kind, soft-spoken man. He walked around into the cage with Mr. Rigney and held out his hand.

"He said, 'Spider, how would you like to be a California Angel? I'll pay you $5,000 to join our organization.'

"I couldn't believe it, Mr. Billy." Spider's eyes were dancing. "He signed me, that second, on the spot. I started to cry right there, shakin' Mr. Autry's hand. I ain't never been so happy in all my life."

"How long were you with them?" Billy wanted to know.

"I stayed in the organization for six years as a player, mostly in the minor leagues, and a few more as a batting coach in the majors. Never wanted to be with anyone else. Finally, when my momma got real sick, I came on home. The money I made in baseball helped me take care of her 'til the day she passed.

"But I will tell you this, Mr. Billy. I live every day not wonderin' if I could have made it in baseball. I found out on my own. My baseball dream gave me several years of pure joy, just bein' a part of what I loved. Most folks don't get any," Spider said sadly.

"I'll tell you somethin' else. Every now and then, when I close my eyes, I can make it all real again. I'm 'bout the luckiest man you're likely to ever meet, and that's the God's truth."

The emotion was building inside Spider again.

"So, you see, Mr. Billy, I *know* where you're at now, and I know where you're tryin' to get to. Take it from old Spider as gospel. *It's the journey that makes your dreams come to life. It's the journey that makes you proud and strong.* You're *already* one of the lucky few, and I'm so happy to know you."

A chill went through Billy that night. In the most unlikely place, he had met a kindred soul. Someone who understood his quest completely. Someone else who knew the chase was not folly.

Spider caddied for Billy that week in Newburgh. They teamed beautifully together, as you might imagine, claiming a victory that produced the largest check he would ever earn in the minor leagues. But, their new friendship would live far longer and provide each of them with deep and lasting value.

And so, on that night in Orlando, the tale Billy told me was not nearly as funny as so many others had been. That night's story had a much greater impact on me. It proved, once again, that inspiration often comes in the most unusual packages. But if one is receptive, inspiration comes nonetheless.

FIVE

In virtually all of our conversations, one topic *always* came up, a young woman back home. She was the oldest child of six who was raised on a dairy farm just outside of Billy's hometown. She had learned to play the piano from her mother and music became her passion early in life. Her parents were industrious, friendly, and generous people. Their humble home was full of love and laughter.

Billy first saw her across the dance floor one night early in their high school years. Her eyes locked on him at about the same time. The connection was so powerful that neither of them had seriously thought about anyone else since.

The more Billy traveled, the more his loneliness ate at him. Her too. I guess, one day, it just got to be too much for both of them.

And so, during one of our long-distance calls, he admitted that although it hadn't been the most practical thing to do, they decided to get married during one of his few visits back home. For a short time, both sets of parents were disappointed that it hadn't been a large, traditional wedding, but those feelings soon evaporated in seeing how perfectly happy they were together.

Billy often said it was his life's greatest decision.

Her name was Anne Billings and, my goodness, she was a stunner. Anne was nearly as tall as Billy, almost 5' 10" and athletic. She had a soft, musical voice. Her face had a "girl next door" kind of beauty and she often wore her long, blond hair in a ponytail. She could also drink a beer and tell a story with the best of them. Her cheerful laugh was infectious, her smile, like an early sunrise, lit every room she entered. She was always a hit at parties, playing the piano and leading everyone in song.

Inside, Anne was a pure and genuine giver. There was no trace of vanity. She had a refreshing, sweet way about her. Her beauty was one thing, but her unassuming manner made her even more attractive. Whenever she talked about Billy however, her eyes would captivate you. They would dance with excitement and unbridled faith.

Anne shared Billy's dreams with a passion that nearly matched his own. In Billy, she would often confide to friends, she had always seen the seeds of greatness and soon she made his dreams her own. She liked to say that he was "her champion in training." Along with his mother, Anne was his greatest source of encouragement and by far the best thing that had ever happened to him. Every time I saw them together, it warmed my heart. She supported his dreams, she understood his sadness, and she completely embraced him. She encouraged him and never let the disappointments that all golfers live with get him down. She filled the hole in his heart and everyone close to him noticed the change. It was remarkable. He was calmer and far more focused. In the purest sense, she had given him the permission to dream.

Dreaming alone can become a heavy burden. But dreaming with a kindred soul can lighten the load. Together, each small step seemed like a victory.

Their few possessions fit neatly inside a small camper that they pulled behind Billy's pickup. Neither of them had ever been happier. They saw their life together as an adventure, believing that somehow, their shared dream would surely come true.

Life on the road would not be easy, however, especially in minor league golf with meager purses and living week-to-week in places few people ever heard of. Long, boring drives from the swamps of Georgia to the cornfields of Illinois, from the insect infested shores of South Carolina to the sweltering heat of east Texas. There was always the same pressure of having to play well just to stay ahead of expenses. Always the same routine in each new small town: find a campground, the local laundromat, and an inexpensive diner.

All went well when Billy played well, but there came long stretches of wildness with the driver that taxed their finances and began to take a toll on Billy's resolve. Anne's belief, however, never waivered.

One night after a particularly erratic round, Billy was grilling hamburgers at their campsite while Anne was preparing the rest of a simple meal inside the camper. He had become more and more silent in the past few weeks as worry began closing in on him like a gathering storm. They ate dinner at their small outside table with little to say.

When they finished, Anne filled Billy's wine glass, leaned in close and kissed him on the cheek. "Let's talk it through," she nearly whispered.

For a few moments, Billy said nothing, staring at the sun setting quickly now under a purple cloud in the western sky. Finally, he turned to her, eyes glistening. "I've let you down," he said with great sadness. "That's what's killing me lately, knowing all you've given up to come chasing around the countryside with me. I've tried everything, Anne, everything I can think of, and I still can't drive the ball in play regularly. I can't keep doing this to you, living in this tin can of a camper with no regular income. You have no life out here, away from your family, your friends, and your music. It's not fair."

She was rubbing the back of his neck and shining one of her loving smiles on him. "You know what I think is not fair?" she asked him gently. He turned to her. "I don't think it would be fair to either of us if we grow old together and someday wonder what our life would have been like if only we had stuck it out a little longer during the tough times. Who can say how close you are to solving this problem, Billy? How will we ever know if we quit?"

Both her hands were now on Billy's cheeks, their faces inches apart. "I love you, Billy. I love who you are. I love what we are doing. This adventure could only be happening to us right now, while we're young. You're concerned about what I've given up to be here, and I love you for that too. But I gave up those things to actually *be here* and I can't imagine giving *this* up, not yet anyhow."

She kissed him gently. "I know this is going to work, I know it in my bones. You are a great player, Billy Thompson. This is what you were born to do. Something good is going to happen if we just don't lose faith. Promise me you'll keep fighting." He nodded.

They held each other close and watched the sun sink out of sight.

Over the next few months, Billy's game improved. Anne had lifted the weight of guilt he carried, and now and then, she would give little pep talks as needed.

One day, Anne suggested to Billy that they might need a bigger camper in a few months. He didn't catch on at first, but then it dawned on him. He nearly burst with the excitement of becoming a dad. Anne was so happy. Her face beamed. They talked every day about what it would be like. Their happiness and the growing maturity that parenthood provides had a positive effect on Billy's play.

In time, little Billy, Jr. was born, and before the little fellow's first birthday, his dad's new, settled lifestyle had helped him finally become a member of the PGA Tour.

I think I was the first person he called after that final, grueling round of Q-School. By then, Billy's father had passed away and his mother and Anne had followed him every step during those final, nerve-wracking six rounds. I remember the excitement in Billy's voice that day. He ended our conversation with the words, "Mom and Anne have been so great, Mike. I've never felt this good in my whole life." Then, his voice trailed off a bit. "I sure wish Dad was here right now."

"I'm sure he is, Billy," I reassured him. "He's probably smiling from ear to ear. And, I'll bet he's very proud of you."

I could hear Billy choking back the tears when our conversation ended. Professional golf is a long, hard, emotional road. He had just cleared one of its highest hurdles. I know I was immensely proud of him, and prouder still of being his friend.

Up to this point in his life, Billy had never considered himself a complete player, nor did anyone else close to the game. However, everyone did agree upon two things.

Billy Thompson was one of the deadliest putters of his generation. There was genuine magic in his soft hands. He was a genius at reading greens and adjusting to varying speeds from course to course. His stroke was long, low and smooth, and the roll he put on each putt was beautiful to watch. Even the ones he missed always looked like they had a chance. His distance control was flawless, laying even the longest of putts dead to the hole. Even he couldn't explain it, but he was grateful for the magic that blessed his game. He knew that only a few players in the history of golf had shared this gift and it humbled him.

Ironically, he was also one of the most unpredictable drivers of a golf ball among his professional peers. Although his hard work had shown honest improvement, some days he was fine, others horrible. As a result, he cautiously selected the tournaments he would enter, making sure that the golf courses were fairly generous off the tee. Billy's iron game was solid enough to get him to virtually any green that his driver would still leave a shot to, so playing on courses that provided extra room off the tee offered a greater chance for success.

During those weeks when he found more than an average number of greens in regulation figures, his phenomenal putting would insure a solid paycheck at week's end. Billy and Anne both continued believing that if he stayed at it long enough, he would eventually solve the riddle of his ragged teeing game. It was this belief that kept the flame of hope burning for both of them and made their nomadic lifestyle from one tournament to the next worth the effort.

SIX

The answer that had eluded him for so long began to take shape a few short weeks before the United States Open would be staged at Inverness in June. It was something that Billy was cautiously excited about. Here's how he found the magic, or maybe, it found him.

Early in that year's PGA Tour schedule, Billy had been fighting through a particularly difficult time, driving the ball so poorly that he missed several cuts and cashed only a few meaningful checks. It began to affect all aspects of his game, even his magnificent putting. Now, with his reserves dwindling and his resolve being tested like never before, something extraordinary was about to happen. Providence was about to tap my friend on the shoulder.

The week prior to the qualifying tournament for the U.S. Open, Billy finally played himself into contention, easily making the cut. A brilliant third round moved him to within three shots of the lead. A national investment company had nicely bolstered that week's purse and Billy stood to take home a very large check, maybe even win, with a solid final round. It looked as though the break they needed had finally arrived.

But in the final round, he once again began hitting errant tee shots into positions that left him no realistic shot at the championship. Ultimately, his wildness produced another dramatic slide down, and finally off the leader board, leaving him to settle for only a modest share of the prize money. Frustrated and dejected like never before, Billy returned to the campground to help Anne prepare for their overnight drive to the next scheduled event. He could not get his father's chilling words, predicting failure, out of his mind.

Along the drive to the campground, Billy's eye caught a faded sign for a driving range that, like its advertisement, had long since seen better days. Believe me, professional golfers *never* consider stopping at roadside driving ranges, not even the newer ones. But Billy felt an irresistible urge that he could not explain. It was compelling, almost compulsive, as if someone else were inside his body slowing the truck, turning onto the gravel road and passing another battered sign, hanging slightly askew that read… *Welcome to Weed Hill.*

Up the hill he drove, shaking his head in wonder, the dusty gravel road throwing up swirls of itself in the rearview mirror. Eventually a poorly maintained shack came into view. The only open window displayed a few bent and misshapen wire buckets, each holding a variety of worn out range balls. The teeing areas had little or no live turf, only threadbare mats lying on uneven ground. Telephone poles, none completely vertical, surrounded the range, holding together patches of rusty screening that sang a baleful song in the wind. The place was virtually deserted and Billy, still in disbelief, was completely mystified at having stopped at such a place.

Against all logic, he placed a few "honor system" dollars in the Mason jar next to the wire baskets, retrieved his clubs from the truck, and began a practice ritual that he had done thousands of times before: short irons first, then working steadily toward the longer clubs. Sadness and frustration settled in again as his father's words cruelly echoed in his mind. He could still hear them as clearly as the night they cut into him.

"You were wrong about me, Dad," he muttered to himself. "I'm gonna prove it…someday." The emptiness these recollections brought was eased somewhat by the exertion. Golf always seemed to rescue him.

Halfway through the bucket, he felt a curious presence, a palpable aura telling him that he was no longer alone. Billy turned to see a weathered old man, eighty-five-year-old Ian McLaughlin, bleached beard, leaning motionless on his walking stick, intently watching. His tweed jacket and billed cap belied the warm day, and he lit and re-lit an ancient pipe made from an old Scottish root. Thick, white smoke swirled into the air. Several spent matches littered the ground.

Billy smiled to acknowledge his presence. The old man nodded and in making a slight waving gesture with his left hand, encouraged him to continue. He studied closely, focused on Billy with eyes as gray as a sunless dawn. Aside from Billy's obvious physical skills, not unlike any he had already witnessed in a thousand other players over the years, McLaughlin sensed something unusual about *this* young man. He wasn't sure what it was, but the feelings were pleasing and strong.

Having saved the best four or five balls for the finish, Billy hit a few of his normal, wayward tee shots and then prepared to leave. The old man slowly rose and approached. After an introduction and a few pleasantries, McLaughlin explained, in his clipped brogue that occasionally sounded like hiccoughs, about his background as a teaching pro at Carnoustie in Scotland for nearly sixty years. After his wife passed away, he had come to this remote place to help his grandson with his not-so-profitable business. His great passion, however, had been as a clubmaker, a skill made obsolete by mass production.

Their conversation soon turned to Billy's goals and aspirations and ultimately to his lack of command with the driver. Billy told him the predictions of failure his father had saddled him with. "Until I solve this problem I have with the driver," Billy told him, "I'm afraid my father may have been right all along." Billy's last few words were strained with emotion.

Sensing the deep frustration that had been building inside the young man for a long time, McLaughlin removed the pipe from the corner of his mouth.

"Wait 'er, lad, fer jest a moment." he said, turning toward the shack. The old man moved slowly. Billy's eyes never left him. After a short while, he emerged from the shack with a decades-old driver tucked under his arm. It was as new as the day it was made.

McLaughlin described, in great detail, the most glorious week of his life. He explained that when the immortal Ben Hogan made his only appearance at the British Open in 1953, he had asked, with great respect for the old man's reputation, if McLaughlin would build him three custom drivers. At the very mention of Hogan, McLaughlin had Billy's immediate and undivided attention.

In stark contrast to Hogan's publicly cold persona, McLaughlin found him to be kind and pleasant, and extremely interested in the old man's craft. At the end of that week, Hogan was crowned the Open champion and he spent an extra day with McLaughlin testing each of the three masterpieces. Of the three, Hogan purchased two.

The third now lay cradled in the old man's gnarled hands and was being offered up for Billy to examine. It had a flawless, pear-shaped, kiln-dried persimmon head, hand rubbed to a gleaming natural oil finish that enhanced the wood's grain. Braided whipping married the head to the steel shaft and protected its wooden hosel. McLaughlin's own personal com-pounds had preserved the original leather grip. Billy handled it with care, never having seen such a beautiful instrument. McLaughlin smiled. "Doosn it feel good in yer 'ans, Belly? Would ye like tae hit some balls weth it?" At first, Billy was reluctant. After all, the last hands to swing this club in earnest were those of his boyhood idol, the incomparable Ben Hogan. McLaughlin insisted, "Get on weth it, lad, ye cana hurt it."

Teeing up a new ball from his bag, Billy carefully wag-gled the club back and forth. As he had done thousands of times before, he took one last look at a distant target and then paused, sensing something nearly spiritual about to happen. He felt his hands molding to the leather, felt the club becom-ing a part of him. From the inside out, a calm came over him and the swing that followed was in ultra slow motion.

Slowly, the clubhead carved a perfect arc in the cloud-less sky. Every muscle stretched to its fullest as his backswing reached its quiet and gentle finish. A slight pause and then the downswing began as his shoulders reversed their rotation. It flowed slowly at first, holding the acute angle between his forearm and the club's shaft. Now like a runaway locomotive gathering fluid energy, his wrists released the angle and ex-ploded the clubhead into the hitting zone. At impact, the club smashed the ball so perfectly that Billy could actually see it flatten against the clubface before rocketing into flight. As his follow-through roared to its athletic finish, his eyes watched the most magnificent tee shot he had ever seen, much less hit. It thundered straight down range, clearing the distant fence, still ascending, and left Weed Hill behind forever.

Another ball, and then another, all identical. Awestruck, Billy could not speak.

McLaughlin smiled, "That wos mogical, Belly. Those wer *grreat* gowf shots." He touched the young pro's shoulder. The connection startled them both. It was electric.

A few more puffs from the weathered pipe. McLaughlin now knew for sure.

He told Billy that he had been waiting all these years to finally meet one *special* player whose dreams would be worthy of owning the club. One player passionate enough to protect it, treasure it, and above all, *"make it sing like the songs in your heart."*

"Aye, Belly, that special pla'r…would be *you*." A chill went down the young pro's back.

Amidst a mild protest from Billy, McLaughlin insisted, "Get on now, lad, she's what ye need," and bestowed the ancient driver upon Billy. The mist in the old man's eyes said what they both realized at the same instant—the gift was not of wood, or steel, or leather...no. This gift represented far more. McLaughlin had just given Billy Thompson the final piece of the puzzle, the magic tool with which to begin building his family's future.

Billy could not have known at the time, but this chance meeting was another of those mysterious moments in his life when, as he prayed for a particular answer, it always appeared in a most unusual way. Surely, someone had to be watching over him.

However, *that particular* answer started a chain reaction that would dictate the remainder of his life. The first important step was qualifying for the U.S. Open a week later. Having found the solution to his game's most frustrating riddle would make that step a surprisingly easy one.

SEVEN

The qualifier for the Open was held in Columbus, Ohio, and an unusual number of PGA Tour players were entered because Jack Nicklaus' tournament at Muirfield was close by in Dublin. A few of Billy's friends had noticed a calm and unusual confidence about him, and those who joined him for practice rounds were speechless in their attempts to describe the length and accuracy of his new, and amazing, driving game.

The golf course, Wedgewood Country Club, was long and tight. The outcome was not. Billy turned in rounds of 64-66 to win the qualifier by four shots. He was going to play in his first United States Open Championship. It didn't seem real. He called McLaughlin to thank him.

"Ye had it in ye all along, Belly. The cloob just set it free," came McLaughlin's response. It was said in such a joyful tone, satisfied completely that his gift had gone to the right man.

The newfound magic had been the key. He and Anne were beyond excited. This was a monumental step forward. They shed tears of joy and excitement and anticipation. Still, they wondered. Would it last? Could it get him through the four grueling days of extremely narrow U.S. Open fairways bordered by the most brutal rough on the year's professional calendar? Time would tell.

Inverness Club was long, mean, lush, and ready. It was laying in wait for all of them.

During the short drive to Toledo, Billy and Anne talked openly about what a solid finish would mean in their lives. It was the exciting kind of "what if" talk, the kind at which all dreamers and young couples excel. Those four days, they thought, could become more important, and potentially more life-altering, than for anyone else in the 156-man field.

Following my own father's death a year or so before, I had been living in the house in which I grew up, on the western edge of Toledo. Naturally, when Billy called me from the qualifying site to share his exciting news, I immediately insisted that he, Anne, and Billy, Jr. spend the week with me. I had plenty of room and the house was only ten minutes from the club. They would have a refuge away from the crowds, little Billy would have a huge backyard and a park nearby to play in, and I would have my friend and his wonderful wife all to myself for the week. They loved the idea. It was perfect.

They arrived later that night. Billy and I had not talked for a couple of weeks. I couldn't wait to hear all about the qualifier. I knew something special had to have happened for Billy to go *that* low on a tight course like Wedgewood. He was a wonderful player, but two or three of his usual "chip-outs" per round didn't normally produce those kinds of numbers. 'He must have putted "lights out,"' I thought.

After Anne got little Billy settled in, I poured one of my favorites, a soft merlot from J. Lohr, and offered a toast from the heart. "Here's to the two best people I know. And, here's to your first of many U.S. Opens. No one deserves this experience more than you two."

There were smiles all around, and finally, I couldn't stand it any longer. "64-66! How the hell did *that* happen?"

Billy started laughing. "I meant to call you all week, Mike, but I didn't want to jinx myself," he said. "I had to know that it was *real* before I told anyone," he confided, almost in a whisper.

"Told anyone *what?*" I begged.

Billy took a slow sip of pure Napa pleasure. The merlot was especially good, but I knew the red wasn't the only thing he was enjoying. The three of us sank into my way-too-soft couch.

"McLaughlin!" Billy began chuckling, "An old man named McLaughlin." Smiling from ear to ear, he took a deep breath and began telling me the remarkable story of his chance meeting with the old Scot. It was almost like hearing about a persistent explorer finally stumbling onto an ancient shipwreck, with gold scattered all about the ocean floor.

It was an amazing tale, one so mystical that I said aloud in amazement, "That sounds almost pre-destined." Billy pursed his lips, and his eyes misted a bit, nodding in agreement. Anne just kept beaming. She may never have been more proud of him.

Billy said without boasting, "Mike, I drove the ball better these past two days than I ever have in my entire life. I could fade it, draw it, hit it long, and hit it *straight*. Whatever I needed for each hole, that's what I was able to do. It was amazing. And it seemed so effortless, almost as if someone else's hands were on that club." He swirled his wine in the long-stemmed crystal, studied it for a moment, then looked up at me, "If it keeps up, my friend, this week's gonna be one helluva ride."

"Oh, and how about *this*, Mike? I called Spider about caddying for me this week. In spite of those old arthritic knees of his, he accepted immediately. He was really excited about the two of us working together again. I called Ralph Howe down in North Carolina and he's going to help Spider get here, probably on Tuesday. Won't that be great?"

The excitement in his eyes was like a man standing at the prison gate knowing his sentence was just about to expire.

EIGHT

Billy arrived at Inverness early Monday morning, well before the majority of players had registered. The reception committee was made up mostly of club members' wives, attractive and friendly. They asked him first to sign the Championship roster that later would be framed and hung in the clubhouse as an autographical snapshot of the Open's field. As is customary, he received a gift from the Inverness members as a memento of his participation in the tournament. The beautiful wool afghan had the Inverness crest woven into it. Next, he signed up for a courtesy driver who would take him to and from the course each day. Finally, one of the gentlemen assigned to locker room duty for the week escorted him to his locker.

The USGA is very democratic with its locker assignments. Every player is simply situated by alphabetical selection. Therefore, Billy would be lockering somewhere close to Lee Trevino, Arnold Palmer, and Gary Player. By now, of course, he knew each of them, and they him. Their relationship was cordial, but as with every journeyman player on tour, he had not come close to reaching their status. In other words, Billy still felt thrilled just to be in their company. His locker location was one of the first things he told me about when I saw him later on the practice range. I *had* to smile. The "little boy" in Billy was never too far from the surface, one of the many reasons he was so engaging.

The next thing he said was, "Wait a few minutes, 'til

I'm warmed up a bit. I've got something to show you." Of course, I remembered our conversation from the night before. I couldn't wait for my first glimpse of the magical driver.

Finally, out of the bag it came. I kept thinking, "It's just a freakin' golf club. What could be so great about it?" But I must admit, when Billy pulled the headcover off, I remember thinking, "it *does* look different, beautiful, in a very simple way." He teed up a ball and gave me the patented Billy Thompson wink.

As he addressed the ball, something remarkable happened. It was as if the atmosphere around us changed. The air seemed clearer, fresher, and much more invigorating. Billy's swing, always a thing of beauty, was so extremely fluid that even the "swoosh" of his downswing was different. And the sound...oh my goodness, the sound that came from contact with the ball. It was indescribable. It was a blast that had other players on the practice range turning their heads in wonder. And the trajectory—long, flat, and straight—was unlike anything I had ever witnessed from Billy, or from few other players I had covered throughout my career. It was only a practice ball, but it was jaw dropping.

Billy looked at me, eyebrows raised as much to say, "See why I'm so excited?"

For a second, I was speechless. "Show me another one," I finally blurted out. He did, again and again.

Finally, he looked up at me. "I told you, Mike," he said, eyebrows raised even further.

It was at that *very* moment, I knew something special was about to happen to my struggling friend. All I could say to him was, "I think this may be your week, Billy."

"Man, wouldn't *that* be something," he said, slapping me on the shoulder.

I picked Spider up at the airport on Tuesday morning. It was easy to pick him out of the long line of arriving passengers. The man was immaculate, and besides, who wears a bow tie and white shirt for a plane trip in June? I also noticed he had a considerable limp as his knees bowed outward with each painful step.

With Billy as our common thread, we were like old friends within seconds of meeting. He was so thrilled to be there. Of course, it was his first U.S. Open as well, and the excitement was obvious.

As we shook hands, Spider's eyes were wide open. His smile was so engaging.

"I am so happy to finally meet you, Spider," I said. "Billy's told me all about your week together in Newburgh. You guys have a lot in common. I'm sure Billy has told you that I am a sports writer, so naturally, I loved hearing your baseball stories and how well the two of you worked together that week. He always speaks so highly of you."

Spider smiled a shy smile. "You know, Mr. Mike, other than most of my baseball career, that week in Newburgh was my favorite sports memory. Mr. Billy ranks as one of the very best men I ever met, in or out of sports. I consider our friendship an honor and a blessing, that's for sure." He sighed, "Ain't nobody deserves this break more than he does. I'll do anything I can to help him this week, you can count on that. I can't wait to see him again."

"I couldn't help noticing your limp, Spider," I said, concerned. "Do you think you'll be OK this week?"

He chuckled, "Done slid too hard into more than my share of second base bags, I guess. Just a little arthritis is all. Nothin' I can't handle."

We chatted like schoolgirls all the way back to the house.

I knew immediately why he and Billy had become so close. He was a warm and genuine man and I liked him right away. There was plenty of room at my place for Spider. It was, as I said, a big old house.

When we arrived, Anne greeted us on the front porch with little Billy. When Spider held out his hand, she gently brushed it aside and gave him a welcoming hug, saying, "I can't tell you how much it means to us, Spider, to have you and Billy back together. After all his stories, I feel like I've known you forever."

Somewhat embarrassed, Spider smiled, "Oh, Miss Anne, it's surely a pleasure to finally meet *you*. Nothin' could've kept me away. Whatever it takes, ol' Spider is here to give it."

Then he looked down at little Billy who was shyly peeking out from behind his mother's skirt. "What a beautiful little man," he said. "I am so happy for you both."

Billy couldn't wait for the practice rounds to be over. He spent the early days of his first U.S. Open week working on his game, polishing the little things. He was definitely under the radar. Most of the media focused on the big name players but Billy liked it that way. Other than a local spot with me, of course, he wasn't called on for any other pre-tournament interviews. Watching it all beginning to unfold, I was amused as the first round approached. "No sense telegraphing an ambush," I whispered to myself.

Little by little as the week progressed, Billy began getting deeper into his own world. I never saw him so calm, so assured, so confident. There were no apparent nerves. It was fun knowing something few others knew. I knew my friend was about to make a serious run at bagging his lifetime dream. The toughest part was the waiting.

NINE

There is a definite pecking order when it comes to generating the pairings in a professional golf tournament. That is especially true in a U.S. Open. The reason, of course, is television, easily the biggest marketing elephant in the room.

The United States Golf Association adheres to the general rule that says if a player is given an early Thursday tee time, he can expect a correspondingly late Friday tee time. The tournament committee then makes sure that a certain number of *marquee* players will be available for the later time slots on each of those days, especially to attract larger television audiences and on-site galleries for both of the first two days. Of course, once the 36-hole cut is made to the low-60 players and ties, the pairings are then dictated by the scoring of the players themselves, with the leaders playing in the last few groups.

However, the more obscure a particular player might be, generally the poorer his times and pairings. Make no mistake. They are *all* good players, since no one qualifies for a U.S. Open without a considerable amount of skill. However, these are players, such as local pros and excellent amateurs, who are virtually unknown outside their own communities. They, and a number of journeyman touring pros, have very little, or no, marketing value. As far as the Championship Committee was concerned, Billy fell nicely into this group. His tee time for Thursday's opening round was early, 7:45 A.M.

There is something fascinating about these "no-namers," however. Nearly every year an obscure player, from out of nowhere, shoots the score of his life and takes, or shares, the first round lead in the Open. It's incredible how often it happens. It's almost traditional. Considering its regularity, I am always amazed at how many people are stunned by the name on top of the leader board following day one of the Open. True to form each year, as if by some secret script written by the gods of golf, that lucky player's fifteen minutes of fame evaporates faster than an August dew. By the end of day two, he's usually gone, rarely heard from again.

United States Opens are always more of a marathon than a sprint. They become a four-day grinding test of will, heart and patience, as much as pure skill. The great players know that their task early on is merely to stay in touch with the lead.

Strategically, it's not much different from running a thoroughbred horse race.

Most often, the "chalk" does not take the lead at the first turn, generally holding back, settling in with the early speed. They wait, with patience and cunning, jockeying for a position from which to strike coming out of the last turn, then going hard to the whip and driving down the stretch to the wire. Golf championships certainly take longer to play out, but the strategy and the drama of horseracing is quite similar.

That is why, to most knowledgeable observers, it was not much of a shock to see Billy Thompson's name on the early leader board. It was, after all, *early.*

Billy made the turn at 3 under par, but instead of fading on the incoming nine, he added three more birdies and a bogey to finish the first round with a 5 under par-66. I followed him a good part of the way, and it was as solid as any round I had ever seen him play. The best part, of course, was his obvious confidence in the McLaughlin driver, and the calming influence of his North Carolina friend. He was rarely in any kind of trouble, making the round seem smooth and effortless.

As the early pace setter, he was in demand for several interviews in the press pavilion. In typical fashion, Billy ducked into one of the corporate tents nearby and made out a large nametag that he slapped onto the front of his shirt before entering the press area. Knowing that there would be many reporters who would not know who he was, he proceeded to go around the room and introduced himself to every member of the press. His big smile and friendly manner took most of them by surprise. His pro-am skills were coming in handy.

Veteran sports writers are generally good people with highly tuned, and wry, senses of humor. But they also have been hardened by athletes with stratospheric egos, the ones who have perfected a public persona that masks who they *really* are. To reporters weary of the sound bites that characterize most interviews with multi-millionaire athletes, Billy Thompson was something new and fresh. He was a genuine guy just trying to dig a career out of the dirt. He was funny and candid, and someone they instantly trusted to give honest and unvarnished glimpses into the struggles and heartbreak of being a striving touring professional on the one hand, and the unlimited joy of the moment he was now living on the other. A moment, most believed, that would fade soon enough.

I knew, years before, that Billy would be a favorite in my world. It was great to finally watch it begin. The difference that separated me from my colleagues, however, was my genuine belief that this was only the beginning, not a brief moment of fame as many surely thought it was. They liked him, a lot. And most genuinely wished him well, hoping, if for no other reason, that they had a new story line to explore. But they had seen it all too many times before. There was no reason for them to believe that Billy would be any different from so many other pretenders to the crown.

TEN

I arrived home to find Anne gazing out of the kitchen window at the backyard where Billy was down on all fours with his son bouncing on his back and giggling the words, "Cowboy, daddy, cowboy." The little boy's favorite time of the day was when his dad would magically transform into a pony.

"He's such an amazing father, Mike," she said, "always kissing and hugging little Billy and telling him how much he loves him. He knows, better than most, how important that is...for both of them. He made a vow to himself years ago that *his* children would never have to wonder." She was beaming now. "God only knows how many grass stains I've cleaned. Each one is a moment they've shared. It always makes me so happy."

That evening, we grilled steaks in the backyard and uncorked an aging, dusty cabernet. Knowing Spider's fondness for good reds made the sharing even more enjoyable. He was beaming. "I love this red, but I don't think anything could taste better than that *score* we put up today," he said, raising his glass in Billy's direction.

Obviously, the excitement of Billy's opening round wove itself in and out of the evening's conversation, but like any other gathering of old friends, there were other things besides golf to discuss. It was a relaxed and fun-filled evening, unusual for a rookie sitting on the first round lead of the U.S. Open. Billy asked Spider to repeat a few of his baseball stories for me and Anne, which he was happy to do. We loved the look in his eyes and the excitement in his voice. That made the stories even more meaningful.

Little Billy had become particularly fond of my golden retriever puppy, Katie, and the feeling was mutual. The two of them played beautifully together and usually succeeded in wearing each other out. Katie instinctively seemed to know that she could not be nearly as rough with little Billy as she was with me. He would throw her ball in the floppy-armed fashion of a three-year-old boy, and as she chased after it, little Billy would often collapse to the ground in laughter. Katie would always bound back for more. Throughout the week, we would often find them curled up together, napping. The boy would have his arms gently around Katie's neck, the golden's long, pink tongue lovingly licking the little fellow's face. Billy and Anne loved watching their son bond with this new, carefree friend.

Billy turned to me and said, "I think dogs are some of God's finest creatures. There's no better way for a youngster to learn more about loyalty and unconditional love than from a dog. Just look at the two of them, Mike. Isn't it wonderful, Spider?"

"It surely is," came Spider's admiring reply. "It surely is."

I nodded in agreement.

Anne was massaging Billy's shoulders. "I wouldn't mind having a nice dog like Katie along with us, Billy. Just look how happy he is," motioning toward the laughter.

Billy concurred immediately. Then, holding both hands on the small of his back in mock pain, he said, "Honey, when this week's over, let's pay a little visit to Katie's breeder. Maybe a nice dog would give our little cowboy's pony a rest." She leaned over and kissed him on the cheek.

Every time I looked at Katie over the years, I thought about *that* conversation. It wasn't a long one, but it stayed in my mind a very long time.

ELEVEN

Two stories dominated the morning headlines.

With the Open claiming valuable real estate in the Sports section, there were a number of the usual bylines. Reporters were always trying to find a different slant to share with their readers. The story of Billy Thompson was a tender one.

My by-line took the reader into the world of a struggling golf pro and his little family, how they managed to keep their spirits and their expectations high in the face of so many disappointments. How they managed to stretch an uneven income and were able to travel week in and week out. How they handled the challenges of raising a young son on the road.

The article paid particular tribute to Anne, to her amazing spirit and to her unshakeable faith in her husband's dreams. I described our long friendship, how steadfast the two of them had been and how happy I was to see good things finally happening for Billy and Anne. I finished with a personal premonition that there was more to come. Some of my colleagues said it was one of the better glimpses inside the non-glamorous side of the sporting world that they had read.

Another disturbing headline was part of a continuing and frightening story. It was one that concerned me a great deal, particularly because it was unfolding in my hometown. For the previous two weeks, there had been a string of random, gang-related armed robberies scattered throughout the city. The robberies had become successively more bold, beginning first with a carry-out at a gas station, then escalating to small grocery stores and a pizza parlor. As they progressed, they became more violent; the worst involved the pistol-whipping of an elderly storeowner just the previous week. But *that* morning's headline screamed from the front page what all of Toledo had begun to fear.

BANK MANAGER GUNNED DOWN IN LATEST HEIST
SCHOOLCHILDREN WITNESS KILLING

A brash hold-up in broad daylight had played out with the murder of a bank executive just outside his local branch in front of a group of elementary children returning home from school. The mayor and his chief of police had been under growing pressure to apprehend these dangerous criminals. Now, a variety of citizens groups were storming city hall, demanding action, and expressing fear for the safety of everyone in the path of this growing menace.

Every city in America suffers at times from serious threats to peace and tranquility. This was simply Toledo's turn. The threat was bad enough, but the timing was terrible for the city's image. Billy said it certainly put the golf tournament, and everything *we* were concerned with that week, into perspective.

The following day, the tournament's second round produced more of the same. Billy, now driving his ball longer and straighter than ever, simply blistered Inverness' front nine. His score of 30 was 5 under par and he backed it up with a solid inward nine of 34 to miss the Open's single day scoring record by one shot. More important, his 12 under par total of 130 was six shots clear of the nearest competitor. He and Spider made it look ridiculously easy.

Billy Thompson was now the halfway leader in the U.S. Open and was threatening to run away and hide. But there were ominous clouds on the horizon. The weather forecast called for a major front to move in overnight, providing another serious challenge.

When I got home, I couldn't wait to hear more about Billy's round. I had been stuck, for the most part, in the press area all afternoon and had followed the action as best I could on television. Billy was on the phone with McLaughlin. He was so excited, talking about the driver and the shots he had been producing with it. He motioned for me to get on the other phone to listen in.

I picked up the receiver just in time to hear McLaughlin say with enthusiasm, "The mogic's in the mon, Belly, not in the cloob. Ah knew ye were the special one, just needn' a bit of a poosh tae bring out the music. The spir't o' gowf is in yer heart, lad. Ah felt thet the first time ah met ye. With that, and the cloob, you'll not be needin' anythen else."

The old man's voice was rising with passion. "Yer goin to do this, Belly, ah can feel it. Ah believe in ye, lad, hunert percent."

When their conversation ended, Billy looked at me from across the room. "God, that old man makes me feel good about myself," he said.

'A feeling *someone else* should have given you a long time ago,' I thought.

TWELVE

On Saturday, as the tournament leader, Billy's tee time was late. At 1:45 P.M., he was paired in the last twosome of the day. To compound the challenge, the weather had turned seriously sour. A steadily increasing drizzle and dropping temperatures were forecast all day. Billy and Spider were destined to get the worst of it. It would be the kind of day that would try any man's patience.

In typical fashion, Billy's first concern was how the cold and wet would affect Spider's knees. We thought if we applied a heavy amount of liniment to each knee and then wrapped them in gauze it could create, and hold, a considerable amount of heat. A pair of wool trousers under a rain suit should also help. That approach, plus an ample supply of aspirin, just might do the trick. Spider agreed, although he felt we were making "too big a fuss" over him. But his limp had gotten progressively worse, and he appreciated our concern.

"As far as the golf, Mike, I'm ready for this kind of day," Billy said. "There will be some of these guys who'll lay down in this kind of weather and that just helps my odds. Remember, pardner, *real* pressure is being two shots outside the cut line with only three holes to go, *and having a car payment due.* I can handle a little rain, especially in an Open." His smile reassured me. Spider was nodding in agreement.

Having traveled the back roads and the backwaters of minor-league golf on nearly every mini-tour, Billy learned how to anticipate and prepare for bad weather. With their own money up for grabs, those guys played every week regardless of the conditions. Those were the days before waterproof rain gear and golf shoes. It was a real struggle to stay dry for an entire eighteen holes. Being cold and wet was miserable and inescapable. The first casualties were often focus and resolve, providing a handy excuse for a poor score.

Billy was known as a good "mudder," but in truth, he was simply a better planner. For one thing, he had one pair of shoes strictly for wet weather. Every week, without fail, he would carefully apply two or three coats of liquid silicone to the soles, the uppers, and especially to all the stitched areas. Those black leather shoes, over time, became as waterproof as a duck's rear end.

He also religiously treated his nylon "rain" suit, both jacket and pants, with spray silicone. Even when brand new, these suits were nothing more than windbreakers, and if left untreated, they couldn't repel water for more than two or three holes. Billy's garments became a *real* rain suit. He even had a special hat that he treated as well. He knew that the longer he could stay dry and relatively comfortable, he would have just that much more advantage over the field.

Billy also carried a hand warmer, a big one. Not the air-activated pouches so popular today, but a large cigarette lighter-type mechanism that actually burned lighter fluid, and was carried inside a felt bag with a drawstring. Warm hands never lost their "touch," but cold ones were death on the short game. He was the first on tour to carry two umbrellas, one for himself, the other for his caddy and clubs. There were always several gloves and towels in his bag, strictly to maintain dry contact between hands and grips. And Billy had learned the art of "layering," making sure the trunk of his body had several layers of light clothing, while his arms moved freely, covered only by the long sleeves of an old cashmere sweater and those of his waterproofed jacket.

He always told me the road to low scoring in bad weather is paved with two things: "warm" and "dry."

As the weather progressively deteriorated during that third round, scoring did as well. The best score on the board had been posted early, a one under par-70. Everyone else, it seemed, was going in the other direction. That 70 was still the benchmark when Billy finished his first nine at even par.

As they started the final nine holes with several steep slopes ahead, Spider continued having difficulty keeping the pace. Billy had noticed it earlier and in an effort to save Spider the embarrassment, he began walking more slowly himself. But it gradually got worse.

Finally, as they stood waiting for the tenth green to clear, Billy turned to his friend and said, "Spider, I know you're really hurting. This is an especially tough day for those old knees of yours. We're still close to the clubhouse, and we can easily get someone out here to finish this round. If you want to go back to the house and rest up for tomorrow, I would perfectly understand. As a matter of fact, that's exactly what I think you should do. I'm worried about you, man."

Spider turned to face Billy. Water was running freely off the front of his cap. He wondered how many men, in the midst of leading a U.S. Open, would even think about their caddy's discomfort.

"Mr. Billy," he said, "I have lived with a lot of pain over the years, physical pain that often tempted me to stop tryin'. Pain in my heart, like when Momma died, that made me think that life hurt too much to go on. But I'm proud of the fact that I never quit on myself."

He was looking Billy straight in the eye now. It was a look that conveyed the admiration that lucky men can have for one another. He laid one hand on Billy's shoulder. "As long as I can put one foot in front of the other, I'll never quit on you either, Mr. Billy, not ever."

Billy gently put his hand on Spider's upper arm. "You're a helluva man, my friend. One *helluva* man."

Spider's commitment, and his courage, filled Billy with inspiration. His fine touch saved several pars on the incoming nine, coupled with three long-range putts for birdies at the tenth, thirteenth and eighteenth holes. His 68 on that miserable day continues to be one of the finest rounds ever played in a U.S. Open, and his total of 15 under par-198 with only one round remaining stretched his improbable lead to a full *eight shots.*

Normally, the press area gets somewhat deserted as a tournament day grinds to its conclusion, especially one as cold and miserable as that day had become. But not *that* day. It was jammed with newspaper and magazine reporters, and radio and television sports anchors from all around the world. Everyone wanted to see Billy Thompson and hear his every description of that day's phenomenal performance. The place was pandemonium before he arrived, and dead quiet when he spoke, his every word being written or recorded. Billy was proud of his round, to be sure, but he was taken slightly aback at everyone's reaction. He had shot several low scores before in terrible weather, but no one had ever been *there* afterwards to make a fuss while he stood alone loading his gear into the trailer after some nondescript mini-tour event.

He answered several questions in his friendly, matter-of-fact fashion. "What was he feeling right then?" one reporter asked.

"Happy to be in out of the rain." Billy replied, bringing laughter to the large room.

"What was your key to scoring on such a miserable day like today?" was another.

"Well, I tried to stay as dry and as warm as I could," he said. "I have the finest caddy in the tournament, and he really took care of me today. The other key was my driving. Hitting fairways in an Open is always important, but with the long rough as wet as it was today, the driver was the most important club in my bag." He paused for a second, thinking fondly of McLaughlin, and added, "and I drove the ball better today than ever before in my life, under any conditions."

"How was your putting?" came another query.

Billy looked at the reporter and, again, a big smile came over his face. "Well, I only needed 26 of 'em, so I'd say it was," he paused, quite pleased with himself, "pretty damn good."

The bright lights matched Billy's smile. The mood was upbeat. He was no longer the journeyman, the "one-day wonder" that most had predicted. Realization quickly filled the room with what I had known all along. Billy Thompson was for real. A new star was rising in their midst.

THIRTEEN

That night, like all the others that week, was a quiet one. Billy liked the refuge that my home provided, the peace and comfort that a house represents. He and Anne and little Billy had spent so much of their last few years in the cramped quarters of their trailer that even the modest surroundings I had to offer felt like heaven to them. Little Billy loved it there, Anne had told me. The dog, the park, everything. They continued to embarrass me with their daily gratitude, but it sure made me feel good.

Spider was helping Anne get little Billy ready for bed upstairs. His knees were still sore, but a long, soaking, hot bath earlier had really helped.

Billy and I, with a glass of wine in hand, walked outside after dinner and talked about all sorts of things. There was something he had not yet discussed with Anne for fear of jinxing himself, but he looked me straight in the eye and said, "I know we're not quite through with this thing yet, Mike, but I can't help thinking about what winning the U.S. Open would mean to the future of my family. Anne has been an absolute rock for *so very* long now. It would be a miracle to finally give her the home she deserves and to reward her for all her faith in me and all she has sacrificed for my dream. And seeing little

Billy this week with Katie, romping around in your big back-yard, well, the road's no longer the place for him."

He gazed off in the distance somewhere. "I suppose it would also settle some things with my dad, you know, even though he's not here to see it. It would mean an awful lot of stuff that we could put behind us and guarantee a lot of wonderful new things to come." His words were bathed in emotion.

I told him not to get too far ahead of himself, to take tomorrow's round one shot at a time, just like always. If he just kept doing what he had been doing, it would all work out. We clinked glasses, and as he turned away, I saw him brush a tear from his eye.

His dreams had taken him and Anne down a long, lonely, hard road and now they were nearly home. I know he sensed, at long last, breaking from the pack on the final turn and now alone in the final stretch, whip at the ready, seeing the finish line clearly ahead.

Once again, I felt especially lucky to be his friend.

FOURTEEN

The final day of Billy's Open dawned crystal clear with only a zephyr of a breeze. The front had passed. The weather was perfect. Everything seemed ideal.

Billy wanted to get to the club a little early and called his courtesy driver. He needed to join Spider, who had already gone ahead. Together, they would reorganize his equipment after yesterday's struggle. Anne would stay back with little Billy and come later, just before his tee time. I needed to get to the press area in the early afternoon as well, and suggested I take Anne with me.

The courtesy car arrived minutes later, driven by an elderly member of the transportation committee. He greeted Billy and Anne warmly as they walked arm-in-arm to the car. Following a good luck kiss, they separated and Billy slipped into the back seat. Anne leaned into the window for one last embrace.

As the car pulled away, the driver casually mentioned that there had been police barricades erected that morning along his normal route back to the club. He would have to take an alternate street, making the trip only a few minutes longer. Something about the notorious gang that had been rampaging the city of late brought the police to an apartment complex nearby. Billy nodded, his mind only on golf.

As the two of them chatted about the tournament, a reporter was broadcasting live over the radio from the scene of the siege. The car radio was on, audible, but not loud. Billy and the driver continued, immersed in their pleasant conversation.

Suddenly, the reporter's voice turned more and more agitated as two members of the gang were apparently escaping through the police line in a large, red pickup truck, smashing a couple of police cruisers as they left. Shots fired could be clearly heard in the background. But, neither Billy nor his driver were paying any attention.

Billy had just finished autographing the old man's committee badge and was handing it back to him as they entered the last intersection before arriving at the club. The traffic signal was clearly green, but suddenly shrill police sirens, loud and closing fast, commanded the last instant of their attention.

Then a flash of red. Glass exploding in every direction. And the horrible thunder of metal melting into metal.

FIFTEEN

Years later, I had a dream about the accident. It was a long, protracted, and extremely vivid dream and one with unusual clarity. It was unlike any I had ever experienced, before or since. Nothing like the disconnected and convoluted stuff of most dreams. I awoke around 4 A.M. and wrote down everything I could recall.

The collision was sudden, shocking, and devastating. Billy's elderly driver sat near the curb, dazed, with minor injuries. At first, Billy was confused and disoriented, but as he began realizing what had happened, he was surprised at feeling no pain at all. The only thing he felt was lucky.

His next sensation, however, was very odd. He was viewing the wreck as if suspended by some invisible wire, detached from the twisted metal, smoke, and shattered glass. He turned and faced the late morning sun. It warmed his cheek, and drew him. He began laughing inside, thinking about people whose hearts had stopped during surgery, then upon being revived, claiming their only memory was one of bright light.

In the distance, he could hear, faintly at first, then growing louder, a brass band. Trumpets? No, bugles—*thousands of bugles*—soothing and beautiful. The music was familiar, triumphant, much like the opening theme from the Olympic Games. He moved closer...closer...and then, suddenly, he *knew.*

His bewilderment turned to sadness, deep, wrenching sadness. What about Anne? Little Billy? Their bright new future?

Gone...all gone. He slumped to the side of the road, feeling an emptiness that he could not possibly describe. Something was terribly wrong. How could this have happened when he was on the verge of having all he had worked for? It had all been so close, so *very* close. The questions bombarded him.

His wrenching sobs stole his breath away. His tears were not just of self-pity, but so much worse. These were tears of sudden, crippling despair as he realized that his family would now be forging ahead without him. Their grief, their emptiness, and all that was lost in an instant, welled up from deep within and flowed down his cheeks, unchecked.

Time...he had no real sense of it now. No telling how long he had sat there, watching an endless parade of souls drawn to the light, and the bugles. They shuffled by, unaware, or at least untouched, by his sorrow. It seemed like minutes. It seemed like forever. Billy never felt so helpless. His heartbreak went beyond devastation.

Then a hand, a gentle, consoling hand, rested lightly on his shoulder, followed by kind words of solace. Words Billy felt as much as he heard.

"I am so very sorry, Mr. Thompson. There has been a terrible mistake. Please, come with me."

SIXTEEN

The stranger took Billy's hand, much like his mother had done on his first day of school. The stranger's face was very kind, his smile genuine. They walked for a while, as if he were dreaming, and entered what appeared to be the main building of a large Ivy League university. Billy was lead to a narrow, comfortable room, wood paneled with tall ceilings. Its furnishings, tapestries, and paintings were exquisite. The stranger, upon reaching the reception desk, whispered to a beautiful woman sitting behind it. She nodded and looked toward Billy, offering a warm and sympathetic smile.

The stranger then returned to Billy's side and said, "I'm going to wait with you until He's ready to see you."

"Who's ready?" inquired Billy.

The stranger hesitated and smiled again, as Billy's face told him that he already knew the answer.

"He's known you before you were conceived, Mr. Thompson. He has known all of us, for all time. His existence often surprises, even shocks, quite a few newcomers, I can assure you."

"What is He like?" asked Billy. "I don't want to offend Him. What should I do...or say?"

The stranger took his hand again.

"His kindness has no boundary. He has infinite patience.

And His depth of love and generosity are beyond *anything* you can imagine. He is really quite amazing, as you will see. Take comfort, He loves you unconditionally, Mr. Thompson, and I know He feels terrible about what has happened. Everything's going to be fine, I assure you."

A few minutes passed. The receptionist finally leaned forward. "Mr. Thompson, you may go in now." The stranger, smiling warmly, wished him well and watched as Billy stepped through a large oak doorway and into the room beyond.

The room was rich and elegant, but surprisingly simple and understated in its décor. It was not nearly as large as one might imagine. The sun shone brightly through a large bay window on the opposite wall, reflecting the rich colors of red oak flooring. In the middle were two opposing leather couches separated by a gleaming walnut coffee table with rosewood inlays.

The kindest, most soothing voice Billy had ever heard beckoned him to approach the couch nearest the window, so the sun would be at Billy's back. Rising from the other couch and extending His hand was a tall, handsome man, who Billy estimated was in his mid-sixties. The sunlight cast gleaming highlights in His silver hair.

"Hello, Billy," He said kindly. "I've admired your spirit for so long, but I must admit, I was hoping you and I would meet *much* later and under much more pleasant circumstances." Billy took His hand and instantly felt at ease. The man's face was spellbinding.

He motioned for Billy to sit, and then continued.

"I know we have the reputation up here for being perfect in all things, and I must say that we do pretty well most of the time, especially considering how big the world has become. Nonetheless, I was saddened to learn of your accident this morning. We had planned for you to get a red traffic signal at that intersection, which of course, would have allowed the police chase to pass you by. Somehow that message got crossed."

His words and their delivery confirmed His sadness. "I feel *terrible* about this, particularly since we had such great things planned for you and Anne." He paused for a moment. "Please trust me when I tell you that I will personally protect and provide for your family for the rest of their days."

Thinking of Anne and his tiny son, Billy's tears began welling up once again and his sadness forced him to reply, "Thank you for that, Sir, but I am...so devastated." Billy was shaking again. "Isn't there some way to reverse this? Can't I just go back and pick up from a minute or so before the accident?"

The man folded His hands on His lap and stared at the floor for quite some time. His own sorrow made His lips quiver slightly. Finally, He looked up at Billy's drawn face and reddened eyes and said with the greatest regret, "That's one thing I cannot do, Billy. When I began this earthly experiment so very long ago, I vowed not to meddle in, or revise its history, even when we made a mess of things at our end. Aside from that, however, I will grant *any* wish you might have...anything at all."

Knowing that Billy was heartbroken by His answer, He reached across and took Billy's hand again to comfort him. "Is there anything *else* I can do to make it up to you?"

Billy thought for a long, extended moment. Then, his eyes rose slowly, and looking the man squarely in the eye...he sighed, still quivering...and made his wish.

"Hum," He said stroking His chin, "*That's* a tough one. But, I have an idea. It will take some time, *and* some doing." He patted Billy's hand gently. "You'll have to be especially patient with me, but I promise you, I'll work very hard to make *that* wish come true."

SEVENTEEN

I was at home with Anne when the call came about the accident. I remember her face turning pale as she dropped the phone and fell to both knees. The shock set in, quickly followed by sobbing so deep it was more of a moan. "No. Oh, please, no."

I picked up the telephone and heard the news. Billy, my wonderful friend, was gone.

The receiver remained at my ear long after the other end had become a dial tone and I peered through the same window as I had the previous night. Three-year-old Billy was laughing and playing with Katie again in the backyard. It would be years before he would understand what happened to his father. I couldn't help thinking that "innocence" just may be God's greatest insulation in times of tragedy.

I spent the next day or two helping Anne make arrangements, a duty that no young wife should ever be required to do. Both of us went through it completely numb.

The funeral was like a "who's who" in professional golf. Tour wives hovered around Anne, offering comfort and sympathy. Several of Billy's friends gave moving eulogies to a man they had known for only a few short years, but loved like a brother. They talked about his generosity when he had nothing, his positive attitude in the midst of struggling, and the unfair timing of his passing when he finally reached the precipice of achieving his life-long dream.

Each said in his own way that knowing Billy Thompson had inspired them to be better men, better husbands, better fathers. They claimed the Tour would never be the same. They were surely right about all those things. The entire golf community, it seemed, mourned his passing and the emptiness of his missed potential.

The night after the funeral, Anne and I were sharing a quiet dinner at my kitchen table. Neither of us ate very much. She had been particularly quiet, a privacy that I did not wish to invade.

Finally, she said, "There's something I want to share with you, Mike," as she slipped an envelope from her purse.

"You were Billy's closest friend on earth and you knew, more than anyone else, what a special man he was. I want to share with you a side of him that I think he only showed to me. I found this under my pillow last Sunday."

I opened the envelope to find a letter he had written to Anne during the last night he would spend with us.

My darling, Anne…

It's about 3 A.M. and I can't sleep. The full moon is softly lighting our room. Tomorrow, God willing, I'll likely become the U.S. Open Champion. But, it is so important for you to know that all the money and all the fame it will bring wouldn't mean a thing if I didn't have you and our beautiful son to share it with.

Sitting here, gazing upon your angel face in the

*half-light, makes me realize that I already have it
all, and nothing will ever change the love I feel for
you tonight.*

*And so, even if tomorrow does not go our way, my
life is already filled to the brim because you chose
to share yours with me. I am at this place and time
because of you.*

*Tonight, I have written a poem for you. I honestly
do not know where it came from, other than from
my soul. I simply touched a pencil to the paper, and
this is what poured out.*

Yours forever,
Billy

On a separate sheet of paper, also in Billy's imperfect
handwriting was the following.

Ours is a oneness
   that defies the limits of definition.
Its mystery lives
   without examination,
   and its love expands
   in its own reflection.

I've shared with you my fears....and you've reassured me.
I've shared with you my thoughts....and you listened.
I've shared with you a simple smile....and you saw my soul.
I've shared with you my heart...and you reflected the warmth.
I've shared with you my pain...and you brought me comfort.
*I've shared with you all my dreams...and you've flown beside
me.*

Our closeness is
> *less a condition than a feeling,*
> *less a body than a spirit,*
> *less a vision than a dream.*

It is less tangible than the air we breathe,
but its fabric is stronger than all its fragile threads.
Its sound, as if crystal, has been sharpened
in the silence of a knowing glance,
> *and sings each day, in awe, of its other half.*

I sat silent for several minutes and then thanked Anne for sharing Billy's last words with me. I held her hand and mumbled something about how lucky we were to have had him in our lives. But mere words could never soothe the sadness that only time could heal.

The water around Billy Thompson had indeed run deeper than most could have imagined.

EIGHTEEN

Anne and little Billy stayed with me for another week but eventually, she moved south. They settled into a small house in Valrico, Florida, just east of Tampa. One of her younger brothers and his wife lived nearby. She found work as a doctor's receptionist and settled into the daily anonymity of raising her precious son. For many years to follow, he would be all that gave meaning to her life. Every day, she looked at him and saw Billy.

With tears in her eyes, Anne had asked if I would like to keep Billy's clubs. I considered that an honor. They sat in the corner of my bedroom for the longest time. I would often look over at the fading name on the bag, *Billy Thompson*. Once in awhile, I would pull a club from his bag and just hold it in my hands, remembering how beautifully *his* hands had molded to it. But it was when I missed him the most that I would slowly slide the McLaughlin driver from the bag and remove the leather headcover. Cradling it always took me back to that first day on the range at Inverness when Billy was so excited to show me the magic that had just completed his game. His enthusiasm and his beautiful smile were always so vivid when I held that club, more so than during any of my other memories of him. But, I only held it once in awhile because my emotions would always get the better of me.

The clubs sat in that corner for a very long time.

The following year, the PGA Tour created a special award in Billy's name. It would be given to the player who had either unselfishly given of himself to others, or who had come from nowhere to make major headlines during that year. Billy had done both.

For many years, Anne agreed to present the award and little Billy was always by her side. But as the years passed, even that small connection to professional golf faded.

As the nomadic atmosphere of the PGA Tour moved from town to town, year after year, the memories of her husband were pushed further into history until a new generation of golfers barely knew who he was, or what he had nearly achieved. It reminded all of us who had known and loved Billy Thompson just how fleeting memories and emotions can sometimes become.

Of course, Anne and I stayed in close touch. My trips to Florida early in each golf season always meant a dinner or two with Anne and little Billy. As every opportunity to see them approached, I counted down the days. With several months between trips, seeing Anne's beauty again always stunned me. Even with sadness in her eyes, she became more beautiful as time went on. When my schedule would permit, I indulged in a day trip to Disney with them, or some quiet time at the beach. Those moments became some of my life's greatest pleasures and memories.

During one of those visits, Anne had asked me to begin telling little Billy about his dad.

I explained the kind of man he was, how much he loved his son, what he had strived for, and what had happened to him. As he grew, I shared more and more of the story. He was always eager to learn more about his father. He could never get enough. All he had were pictures, some magazine articles, and our stories. In his mind and in time, the father he never knew became a giant, a vision I fostered. I knew that Billy had succeeded despite the lack of positive encouragement from his own father, and that he had begun raising his own son in an entirely different way. But now he would not be there to inspire and energize his *son's* dreams. That would become my role and one I accepted gladly.

Once in awhile, Anne and I would have some quiet time together, just the two of us, to talk and console. Inevitably, the conversations would return to our wonderful memories of Billy, and what might have been for the three of them. Anne publicly projected strength, courage, and independence, so little Billy would have a positive atmosphere in which to grow. But each time we had our little private talks, the sadness and her heavy heart were never far from view. I looked forward, more and more, to every phone call and visit, although each broke my heart a little more.

I don't know when it happened exactly, but somewhere along the way, I realized I had fallen in love with her. It felt so strange. I could not shake the feeling that somehow I was cheating on my old friend. So I made a silent vow to him that I would hide those feelings as best I could, while still watching over her and his growing son. It was a very tough choice, but one I felt I owed him. I decided never to tell her.

NINETEEN

Over the years, as little Billy grew, he became Billy, Jr. That was soon shortened to just "Junior." Then, sometime early in high school, his friends further shortened "Junior" and began calling him "JR," a nickname that stuck with him from then on.

During one of our long-distance talks, Anne mentioned that JR started working part-time at Bloomingdale Golfers Club not far from her home, picking up range balls, washing carts, and doing other odd jobs around the course.

I knew about Bloomingdale. It was an amazing place in those days. Touring professionals at various levels of their careers were not only welcomed at that club, but they were encouraged to practice and play there throughout the winter months as they prepared for the tournament season that would scatter them throughout the country all summer.

Bloomingdale's head pro, Tim Fennell, had taken quite a liking to JR, as did several of the nearly one hundred aspiring pros who called Bloomingdale their winter home. JR had his mother's good looks and sweet disposition. He had his father's smile and sense of humor with an endearing shyness blended in. A winning combination to be sure.

On slow days, when all his chores were finished, JR practiced his own game at the far end of the range. Many times,

Fennell would slip out back for a while to help JR with the fundamentals of proper stance, grip, and alignment. Tim and his wife, Ruth, had no children of their own, so he watched over JR and tutored him as if he was his own son.

He had told Anne early on that he recognized amazing natural talent in young JR, that his swing was especially powerful and rhythmic for a lanky young teenager. What excited him the most, however, was JR's passion to learn. The fire inside the youngster was already burning hot. Several of the touring pros saw it too and a number of them had begun offering JR a tip or two.

In the beginning, Fennell had not made the connection between JR Thompson and Billy Thompson. That knowledge would come later in a casual conversation with Anne, and it would explain a lot of JR's ambition. Initially, all he knew was there was something *very* special about JR, something almost beyond his control that commanded his attention and compelled him to nurture this special boy.

Bloomingdale was the perfect atmosphere for JR. He was surrounded by other young men, all striving to excel at a game that is extremely difficult to play well. He saw, every day, the dedication and relentless hard work needed to reach the lofty goals that had already begun formulating in his mind ever since our earliest talks.

JR spent his early teens practicing and playing...and dreaming. He devoured golf. Golf, in turn, loved him back unconditionally. He began to understand his father's unlimited love for the game because those feelings were rapidly developing within him as well. He told me that golf made him feel even closer to his dad and made him appreciate even more what had driven Billy through the dark days before meeting McLaughlin. Just like his dad, golf was in his blood.

His body grew tall, strong, and supple. His perfectly balanced and natural swing was, from day one, dead on plane, and it produced effortless golf shots that left most of the veterans around him shaking their heads in wonder. He also knew every statistic in the game. His mind became an encyclopedia on golf's four major championships: the Masters, the U.S. Open, the British Open, and the PGA Championship. Of these four, the *U.S. Open* became an obsession.

I remember a sunny, hot afternoon when JR and I played nine holes together at Bloomingdale. He was about fourteen at the time. He had just hit a towering three-iron into the long par-3 seventh to about six feet, and he casually turned to me and said, "You know, Uncle Mike, someday I'm going to win the U.S. Open for my dad." He spoke so matter-of-factly, as if he could already see the future as something real, just waiting to happen.

I also remember not being surprised and replied, "I believe you, JR. I can't wait to see it happen. And I'll bet neither can your dad."

He smiled, obviously liking the thought of his father's approval.

When I arrived back in Toledo, an invitation from Inverness' president lay atop my usual large stack of mail. The club was celebrating the opening of their newly renovated locker room, and had invited a number of golf writers to attend. Normally, such an event would pass without fanfare, but Inverness' famous locker room was very different indeed.

From the club's beginning in 1903, Inverness meticulously preserved every piece of its remarkable history. A tour of its two-story locker room could take the better part of an afternoon and will create the sense of being in a very special place. It is actually a golf museum, beginning with pictures of its three clubhouses, the first two of which were consumed by fire in the early 1900s.

Pictures from the first U.S. Open at Inverness in 1920 reveal an entirely different course from the one played today. The property then was nearly barren with few trees, and the photographs reveal Ross' genius of bunker placement and impressive design.

Photographs with personal notes from the game's greatest players are displayed throughout. The career highlights of the club's greatest professional, the incomparable Byron Nelson, and one of America's finest amateurs, Frank Stranahan, are chronicled there.

In the '40s and '50s, Inverness hosted the famous "Inverness Invitational," which drew the top players from around the world and each of those events is heralded with photographs, autographs, and scorecards. There are sequence photographs of Bob Tway holing his greenside bunker shot at the eighteenth to snatch the 1986 PGA Championship from Greg Norman. Beautifully articulate letters to the club from Bob Jones and Jack Nicklaus heap praise on the grand old course.

All there, every scrap of the club's tradition. Magnificent.

Somewhere in that whirlwind of their history, it struck me that hallowed golf ground is consecrated by the *events* that have been staged there, by the great *players* it has challenged, and by the brilliant *moments* they chiseled into golf lore. One need only think of Augusta National, Pebble Beach, and St. Andrews to realize the truth of that thought. It was then I realized that Inverness might have an interest in Billy's clubs. It would be the perfect place, I thought, for them to finally rest. The offer was met with great enthusiasm.

Today in a lighted glass case, every club, including the

McLaughlin driver, is on display. The club asked if I would pen a tribute to Billy's glorious three rounds of U.S. Open golf on their grounds. Those words are engraved on a brass plate that accompanies the exhibit. I am a professional writer. It was my proudest assignment and the most privileged.

> Unheralded Billy Thompson came to Inverness and played the most inspired 54 holes in the history of the United States Open Championship. His eight-shot lead went unfulfilled when a tragic accident took his life on the morning of the fourth round.
>
> In these clubs lives his indomitable spirit. Billy Thompson was a man who embodied the essence of the game and became a lasting symbol of the kind of people golf produces. He was a champion as a golfer, and especially, as a man.

TWENTY

Back at Bloomingdale, Tim Fennell encouraged several of the pros to let JR play practice rounds with them. Some of them grumbled initially about including a kid in their games. After all, they were professionals and he was just a bag boy. Those who did include him, however, were amazed at his mature and competitive nature as well as the low rounds he had begun recording. Soon, they sought him out when making their foursomes, scrambling to have him as a partner. Many were at least ten years older than JR, but it got to the point where none of them could beat him. It was amazing to watch the speed at which his game, and his body, grew.

Everything grew, except his ego. 'Just like his dad,' I thought. 'All of his spikes still planted firmly on solid ground.' God, I was proud of that boy. Always have been. But it also hurt, knowing what Billy was missing.

Fennell believed that JR's education would not be complete until he experienced firsthand everything that a professional golfer must contend with in order to succeed. He would have to learn that there was more to championship golf than just excellent ball-striking in a friendly atmosphere, on a familiar course. He would have to learn about course management, strategy, and developing the arsenal required to carry out the plan. He would have to learn how to adjust when the weather turned sour. No place on earth was better for learning how to play in the wind or on difficult Bermuda grass than Florida.

The next step would involve playing, or at least caddying, in tournament conditions to advance his education. He would then see how frustration could easily turn into anger during a tournament round, and how anger, misdirected, would usually destroy a performance. In short, he would need to learn how to manage *himself*, the most stubborn opponent in golf, not just the mechanical aspects of the game. Fennell, convinced of where the boy was headed, would make sure that JR would be complete, and ready, when he finally got there.

TWENTY-ONE

A lthough his 6' 5" athletic frame was impressive, Fennell's game was solid but not tour quality. His entire life had been spent in the atmosphere of golf's highest level, studying the special skills of many fine players. He had a genius for recognizing a player's strengths and weaknesses and then developing a plan to reach his goals. He loved being exactly who he had always wanted to be, the head professional at a unique club that celebrated and nourished excellence.

Many professionals began their careers while training at Bloomingdale. Fennell had helped several of them polish their games until they were good enough to play on the PGA Tour. They all loved and respected this soft-spoken, unselfish, gentle giant. He took great personal satisfaction in helping others succeed. They all respected and admired him.

Because his intense interest in JR had become a personal crusade, Tim Fennell and I became close friends. We talked at least once a week, no matter where my work took me. These were part of my regular "JR updates." The other reports came from Anne. Whenever I was in Tampa, I would look forward to my stops at Bloomingdale, usually to share lunch with Tim and hear the latest.

When I asked the usual question, "How's JR doing?" during one of those visits, Tim paused, and then, as if gazing at something wonderful in the distance, he offered the following.

"Mike, if you bring me a youngster with good physical skills, I'll turn him into a solid ball-striker," he said. "And, if you bring me a youngster with good physical skills and *intelligence*, I'll make him into a solid player. But," he paused, his voice slowing for effect, "if you bring me a youngster with good physical skills, intelligence, *and a heart bursting with passion*, I will turn him into a *champion*. I'm sure you know, as close to golf as you are each week, that discovering all three of those qualities in *one* person is extremely rare. For a teacher like me, it may only come once in a lifetime."

He leaned closer and said in a near whisper, "I have absolutely no doubt, Mike, *JR is all three. He is beyond special.*"

With a lump in his throat, Fennell was sharing with me what he had silently known for quite some time. He was training a *thoroughbred*.

TWENTY-TWO

Sometime during JR's third year at Bloomingdale, a young man arrived at the club in mid-September. He had graduated from the Ohio State University earlier in the year, turned pro and had knocked around the various mini-tours and state Opens throughout the summer. The stories of his talent were already beginning to circulate throughout the inner circles of golf.

I interviewed him during the week he won the Ohio Open in Canton, Ohio that July. When he learned that I was a Buckeye alum, and covered the PGA Tour most of the year, he asked my advice about preparing for Q-School north of Tampa that October.

"The very best place, in my opinion," I told him, "is Bloomingdale Golfers Club. The facilities are great and the atmosphere is perfect for someone as serious as you are." I gave him Tim Fennell's phone number. I also asked that he introduce himself to JR, and I told him just a little bit of history. "I think he's going to be a fine player someday, and he might be an excellent caddy for you at Q-School," I offered. "Play with him, and let me know what you think."

The young pro thanked me, promising that he would.

His eyes were piercing, his handshake like steel. His name was Adam King.

TWENTY-THREE

From the minute King showed up at Bloomingdale, everyone knew he was different. He was a friendly enough kind of person, but he was extremely focused and deadly serious about his mission. He stayed clear of the little groups of young pros who would often stand around and joke with each other on the practice range to break the monotony. He always went to the far end of the teeing ground for his work. His practice rounds were generally alone, or sometimes with one or two of the other serious players. For all to see, he carried himself as if he already knew his destiny.

Often, his practice sessions drew small groups to watch, silently in awe. From the beginning, everyone knew that Adam King was a gifted and wonderful player. His short game was phenomenal and few could remember seeing a better putter. His practice rounds were surgical, approached as if each was the last day of a major championship. His instincts told him when to attack, and when to play conservatively.

They *all* knew this player was in a different league. He was brilliant.

True to his word, King asked to meet JR and instantly liked him, as I predicted. He was impressed with JR's maturity and his ball striking. Once in awhile, he would include him for a practice round. He liked what he saw. Eventually, they began talking about the looming grind of PGA Tour Q-School. King had begun seriously thinking about having JR on the bag, not only as a favor to me, but because he felt strongly that JR would be a genuine asset. By then, at sixteen, JR already had an advanced grasp of the game and they thought a lot alike. Unlike any teenager King had known, JR was as calm, as unflappable, and as cool-headed as most seasoned pros. He would be much more than just a caddy. He would be a solid teammate. All it took was asking. JR was definitely on board.

Of course, Anne would have to give her approval. She called for my advice.

"He's awfully young to be gone for an entire week, Mike," she said. "He's got school. And, I don't know this Adam King very well, although Tim Fennell speaks highly of him."

I told her, "Anne, he's only going to be an hour away, in Brooksville. I think it would be a great experience for him and everything I know and have heard about King is all positive. Besides, you and I both know where JR's headed. He's going to learn a lot from this experience. Plus, his principal and golf coach both belong to Bloomingdale. Tim won't have any trouble convincing *them*."

Then, to put an exclamation point on my endorsement, I asked Anne, "What do you think *Billy* would say to such an opportunity?"

She paused and I could almost hear her start to smile at the other end of the telephone. "OK, I'll tell him."

Anne knew deep inside that the time was coming when golf would nudge JR out of the nest and into full flight. Best to let it happened gradually, one step at a time, close to home. *That* step, she was now assured, would be a very good one for him.

From that moment on, King's practice rounds were purely singular, just him, with JR on the bag. In return, King joined Fennell in teaching JR a myriad of shots around the short game range. They worked especially hard on his putting. JR had inherited a lot from each of his parents, but unfortunately *not* his father's magic touch. Their games, it turned out, had become mirror images. JR was a wonderfully gifted ball-striker; his father had been a phenomenal putter. Neither of them was complete.

TWENTY-FOUR

The finals at Q-School that year were held at World Woods Golf Club, 50 miles north of Tampa, near the small town of Brooksville, Florida. World Woods boasts of two Tom Fazio designed masterpieces, Pine Barrens and Rolling Oaks. Nowhere has one piece of property produced two eighteen-hole golf courses of such quality that were more distinctly different from each other. Both are extremely challenging.

Pine Barrens is reminiscent of the great Pine Valley course in New Jersey with its sweeping fairways woven through wild, wind-driven waste areas and scraggy dunes. Rolling Oaks is more of a parklands course, emerald green, routed through forests of live oak and around numerous water features. The club's 20-acre practice range allows a player to work on his game in any wind direction and its multiple target greens provide a real course atmosphere. The large putting greens, nine-hole executive course, and three practice holes were perfect for serious preparation. JR had never seen anything like it. The wide-eyed teen was in golf heaven. King was in what most players considered golf hell, Q-School.

The six-round tournament would be played on both courses. The top 35 players in the 150-man field would earn their way onto the PGA Tour. The others would earn spots on the Nationwide Tour, at that time golf's version of Triple-A baseball. The next six days would be full of stomach cramps, nail biting, and seemingly endless hours of scoreboard watching for anyone in contention. It would *not* be that way for Adam King.

The first day dawned cool and rainy. After a nervous first nine holes of 2 over par-38 on the Pine Barrens course, King settled into his machine-like precision. A 4 under par-32 on the inward nine produced a solid 70, the highest score he would record for the week.

The weather steadily warmed, and so did King. By the end of Q-School, his (70-68-69-66-67-68) 408 total of 24 under par led the field by an incredible 10 shots.

The newest member of the PGA Tour had put on a clinic of course management, strategy, personal control and shot-making precision. As anyone at Bloomingdale would have predicted, King displayed pure genius. Of course, the best part was that JR had seen it at close range, felt it, and breathed it.

King had earlier promised Fennell that after each round, he would sit down with JR and review the entire day's work, shot for shot and answer any questions JR might have. Fennell wanted JR to make the most of his opportunity to witness strategy and course management up close. Aside from watching each round at Adam's side, JR learned when to lay up off the tee, how to calculate the odds of gunning for a par-5 in two shots, and playing to specific sides of the pin for the best chances of making birdies. King continued to preach about "staying in the present," that the *only* golf shot ever worth his focus "was the *next* one." Hearing it was one thing, but seeing it done made quite another impression.

JR was already an accomplished ball-striker, with his strong, agile body growing ever stronger as time went on. His physical game grew along with it. But those six days with Adam King had been his personal primer on the mental side of golf, the side few golfers learn without vast experience and through maturity. Everything King did was cool and calculated. He was ready for all that World Woods could throw at him.

When JR remarked at dinner on the fifth night about how he admired this ability in King, Adam shared something that JR had never heard before. King shared what he called "the first two rules of metaphysics."

He motioned for JR to slide his chair closer. He leaned in and spoke low, wanting to share two of golf's greatest secrets with JR alone, and with no one else.

"First, **You must accept things as they are, not as you want them to be.**

"Golf is played outdoors, JR. The weather will not always be pleasant. Golf courses will not always be in excellent condition. You will not always be paired with friends. Luck will not always be good."
He continued, "Great players are always prepared to handle adversity, and they concern themselves with *only* those things they can actually control. They anticipate. They prepare. *They accept things as they are.*

"Second, **Ultimately, you are responsible for everything that happens to you.**

"When a bad break comes your way, remember, no one *else* hit your ball into that situation. Make sure you have practiced bad lies from old divots, tall grass, hillsides, because they are going to happen at the most critical times during a tournament,

I guarantee it. Don't take anything, even the shortest putt, for granted." King raised his index finger to make his point. *"Champions never make excuses, ever.* Accepting responsibility is the first step to being in control.

"Armed with these two rules," King told JR, "you will be well on your way to mental toughness. And," he added, "when you have *that,* you'll be way ahead of the guys you're playing against." JR's brain was recording every word, every lesson.

King leaned back in his chair and wiped his mouth with his napkin. "You're already a fine player, JR, gifted, *truly* gifted. And, as good a ball striker as you are, if you get mentally tough, I mean *really* tough, you're going to be a bitch to beat."

It was like a six-day Masters degree for JR. He missed nothing.

TWENTY-FIVE

In the two months between his victory at Q-School and the start of the PGA Tour schedule in Hawaii, King spent his days at Bloomingdale practicing for the next exciting chapter in his life. Wherever he was, JR was not far away. King wanted it that way. He had precious little time left to teach and encourage his new, young friend.

He had also settled on a business agent, and it was an easy choice. His college roommate, who had recently passed the bar exam, had just gone to work for IMG in Cleveland, possibly the largest sports agency in the business. This young man had been a decent player himself and the shrewd management at IMG made sure he tended to every one of Adam's needs. All sorts of corporate clients were lining up with endorsement contracts, trying to capitalize on the handsome young man who everyone in golf predicted would be the next major tour star.

King took it all in stride and to his great credit, continued helping JR work on his short game and putting. Fennell told me that he had seen a number of young, talented players become very self-centered and aloof after making it to the PGA Tour, but not King. We both felt considerable gratitude for the relationship that had blossomed between them and the inordinate amount of time Adam was sharing with the young man still under our wings. In only a few short months, King had become the big brother that JR never had, and it was heart-warming to watch those two together.

The day came when King would leave Bloomingdale to begin his meteoric rise to fame and fortune. I just happened to be at Bloomingdale that day and was helping JR load the last of King's gear into the car before JR drove him to the airport.

King had always been in complete command of every situation in which I had ever seen him. But on this day, as he turned to say goodbye, his eyes glistened and he swallowed hard. I held out my hand, but instead of taking it, he threw both of his arms around my neck and hugged me, hard.

"I will never be able to thank you enough for guiding me to this wonderful club, Mike," he said. "No matter where I go, Bloomingdale will always have a piece of my heart and whenever I think about this place, there will be three faces in my mind—yours, the pros' pro, Tim Fennell, and this wonderful young man, my new best friend, JR. Take good care of him for me."

The energy in his words uncovered a side of him I had never seen before and it made me like him even more. "Now," he said smiling, "I'd better go out and make as much money as I can before he gets out there to kick my ass."

I watched the car pull away toward the club's gated entrance. Inside were my two favorite young men on the face of the earth. There had only been one other time in my life when I felt I could see clearly into the future. The first was just before Billy's Open, years ago. Then at that very moment, I knew, possibly more than anyone, the mountains that Adam would surely climb and what he would mean in a very short time to golf. I also knew the tremendous impact he had already had on my "surrogate son."

I said a silent prayer for Adam's safe passage and an extra "thank you" to God for rubbing their lives together and fueling the fire already burning inside of JR. In their few short months side by side, JR left his boyhood behind and the young man who was emerging was truly a remarkable sight.

TWENTY-SIX

I n the months to come, King would rocket to the top of the PGA Tour's money list. He won in only his fourth start, at Tuscon, dedicating his first victory to his "little brother, JR," back in Florida. Then, at the AT&T at Pebble Beach a few weeks later, he blistered the three-course rotation in 22 under par for his second win in only six starts, earning well over $1 million in the process. It was *happening*, much faster than even I had any reason to imagine. The phenomenon of Adam King was already raising the bar, setting standards for the rest of the tour to chase. His star status was nearly off the charts.

JR, of course, was ecstatic. He and I talked several times during each week, recapping King's exploits of that particular day. It seemed like each conversation had something new and special to cover. Adam kept in regular contact with him as well. JR's seventeenth birthday was approaching and he could already see himself as a tour player. Now he had the perfect hero to emulate.

Fennell knew that JR would be too distracted to finish all his duties on the weekends and still have time to watch his friend do great things on television. So his creative solution was to have the golf course superintendent train JR in the art of bunker raking and greens mowing. These would be his new weekend jobs. They called for a much earlier arrival at the club, but the new work also allowed him to finish and still get in a few hours of practice before becoming glued to the telecasts in Tim's office.

It gave the young man a new appreciation for the hard work of golf course maintenance and he learned not to take excellent conditions for granted. JR accepted the stick and got the carrot. Weekend days were long and productive, but happy.

Without his father, JR could not have had better role models than Tim Fennell and Adam King. Those relationships motivated him beyond anything that Anne or I could have created. JR now craved competition, and soon began winning every high school event and junior tournament he entered.

One of the kids on JR's golf team was an Irish string bean by the name of Johnny O'Hara. Johnny was a carefree class clown who never took much of anything very seriously. He was a decent high school player, able to break 80 some of the time, a solid fifth or sixth man whom everybody enjoyed being around. Johnny was one of those naturally funny guys who could make you laugh by reciting the menu at Wendy's.

JR talked to Fennell about the possibility of part-time work at Bloomingdale for his pal. Like JR, Fennell started Johnny in the cart barn, washing golf carts and shagging balls on the range. The two boys practiced and played together whenever they could. Before long, they were inseparable.

Johnny recognized immediately that JR's golf was in a completely different stratosphere and he appreciated that it didn't affect their friendship. They were very tight, real buddies. Eventually, Johnny suggested that he caddy for JR in tournaments. He too had a good handle on where JR was headed.

"That'd be great," JR said, sealing the deal. Right then, Johnny became the only regular caddy JR ever had. That seemingly innocent conversation would eventually make Johnny O'Hara a very rich man.

TWENTY-SEVEN

At seventeen, JR played in only his second Florida Amateur Championship, and won handily. The best part about the win, he told me excitedly, was sharing it with Johnny at his side and later telling Adam on the telephone.

That year he also finished fourth in the Florida State Open against some of the finest pros and amateurs in the country. People throughout the state took notice of our tall, lanky bomber. Colleges from all over America showered him and Anne with scholarship offers. It was like watching the best quarterback in the country go through the recruiting process, hectic but exciting.

Anne called me one night just after the golf coach from the University of Florida had visited with her and JR. A full scholarship (tuition, books, room and board), at a great university and one of the country's perennial golf powerhouses was on the table for his taking. However, Anne lamented that JR was not interested in college. He wanted to turn pro immediately. This was something I sensed coming.

Of course, most people's immediate reaction would be to grab the scholarship offer. Four years of college was critical for virtually any career, but it is also a chance for growth in social skills and maturity. I knew how mature JR already was and how dedicated and singular minded he had become about golf as a profession. I also knew that he would be extremely successful financially, regardless of which direction he took. I promised Anne that I would talk with him.

That week, as it turned out, I was scheduled to cover the Memorial in Columbus. Adam and I had already made plans for dinner during that week. I wanted his input about JR's upcoming decision. I was glad I talked with him.

King possessed a wisdom far beyond his years. It was refreshing, too, to see that fame and a rapidly growing fortune had not changed him much. He had always been sure of himself, not in an obnoxious way, but more in a manner that exuded a defined path in life. I admired, and even slightly envied, his ability to see things so clearly. And, of course, he couldn't wait to hear the latest news about JR.

I explained the recruiting frenzy, which did not surprise him. "What does JR think about college?" he asked, already knowing the answer.

I smiled, "What do *you* think, Adam?" We both nodded, chuckling. "I told his mother that I would kick it around with you and Tim Fennell. Between the four of us, I told her, we should be able to help advise JR."

King didn't need much time to reply.

"The Tour is not going away, Mike. It'll be there when JR is ready, one way or the other. You and I both know he'll be very successful whenever he comes out and I'm already looking forward to the day he arrives. Hell, I miss our practice rounds together."

King was rubbing his chin now.

"But, I hope you don't mind my saying so, Mike…JR has been sheltered. Don't get me wrong, it's been the *good* kind. Bloomingdale, Fennell, you, his mom, and golf, all wonderful comfort zones, probably the best thing for a young man like him. He's been the better for it, believe me. But I think college would do more for JR than a lot of other kids. Not just the education, but socially, emotionally. I think he needs to grow a little more in that regard. God knows not as a golfer, he's good enough right now," King said with his eyebrows raised. "But you know what a grind the Tour is, Mike. I'd like to see him stretch out a little, have some fun. Even if he only sticks it out for two or three years, it will be a lot better than if he turns pro right out of high school."

King lifted his wine glass, which had reached the critical refill level. "Would Anne like me to talk with him?"

"She'd appreciate your input." I said. "She knows JR respects your advice." We shook hands and finished another glass of Cline red zin.

Anne told me that when JR got off the telephone with Adam a few days later, he turned to her and asked matter-of-factly, "Mom, do you have the coach's number at Florida?"

And that was that.

TWENTY-EIGHT

J R had been away to school for a couple of years when I got one of my regular phone calls from Anne. By now I had become proud of myself for dutifully watching over her and JR without, I thought, the slightest hint of my true feelings for her. We had always been affectionate, even when Billy was still with us. That continued over the years, until I simply accepted that *that* kind of love was all I could expect between us.

Anne was curious about my schedule. When I replied that it would be at least another month before I was due in Tampa, she seemed quite disappointed.

"That long?" she asked. "I was hoping it could be *much* sooner."

"Why?" I asked, thinking it had something to do with JR.

"Oh, it's nothing, really." she said. "It's just that they've opened a new addition at Berns Steakhouse and they're celebrating the opening by offering some of Berns' favorite reds from his private cellar. Naturally, I thought how much you would enjoy that."

Anne knew my passion for excellent red wine. No place in

America has anything remotely close to the size, or selection, of the wine list at Berns. It also happens to be one of the finest restaurants *anywhere*. An evening at Berns, with its tuxedoed waiters, baroque decor and a menu filled with aged, prime beef, was always an occasion I looked forward to weeks in advance. It is a large restaurant with many small, intimate rooms that further enhance the experience.

Instantly changing my schedule, I said with enthusiasm, "How about this coming Saturday night?"

"I'll make a reservation for seven o'clock, Mike," she replied. I thought I detected excitement in her voice when she added, "Just the two of us."

I tried desperately not to read anything into her tone, but my heart skipped a beat.

The following Saturday evening, I picked Anne up around six o'clock. She was radiant, and tanned. She was simply a vision. Stunning really. She was particularly chatty on our drive into the city and I thought to myself how much I had always relished her company. Every outing was a treat. That night seemed more so.

We had a lovely time at dinner. Anne had chosen one of Berns' smaller rooms, with only about six tables, and began filling me in on the latest news from JR. Florida had just won another collegiate tournament and he had been the medallist yet again.

A little more small talk followed. Then she said, nervously, "I have something to discuss with you, Mike. I have rehearsed this so many times and now that we're together, I am more nervous than I thought I'd ever be." She emptied the last bit of cabernet in her glass and took a deep breath. I leaned closer.

"The last several months," she paused, "I've been dating."

Her words cut through me like a razor and chills went down my back. I knew all along that this day would come, and quite frankly, I had been lucky for much longer than I deserved, not having to share her with someone else. It was purely selfish on my part, but I couldn't help feeling numb. I bolstered myself to fake enthusiasm and support for this new man in her life. But I hated what was coming.

"I'm so sorry, Mike," she said. "I can see that I've upset you. Maybe we shouldn't talk about this now. Maybe you need a little time to get used to the idea." She reached across the table and touched my hand to comfort me.

"No, no. Let's talk about it, Anne." I said, trying to keep my true feelings from being too obvious. I didn't want to spoil something that she seemed so excited about. "I knew it was bound to happen, sooner or later. As wonderful as you are, I'm surprised some lucky man hasn't come along, way before now, to sweep you off your feet."

"Do you think someone would be lucky to have me, Mike?" she smiled.

"Absolutely. Can't wait to meet him," I lied.

She continued, "Dating made me realize what I should have known long ago, Mike."

"What's that?" I asked, preparing for the worst.

Her answer floored me.

"I've thought long and hard about this." Her face was aglow now. "It's been almost twenty years that I've been alone, far too long. I finally concluded that Billy would be thrilled to see you and me together, as a couple. How would you feel about that?"

My heart pounded. My breathing went into double-quick.

The chills came back and my eyes watered. It took a moment for me to speak. I was stunned. All that came out was, "Please, Anne, tell me that you're serious."

She rose from her seat and stepped to my side. Then, Anne Thompson, the secret love of my life, leaned down and gently kissed me. "I'm in love with you, Mike, and I'd love it even more if somehow we could be together."

I stood up and drew her close to me, tears streaming down my face. "I'm the second man on this earth whose dreams you've made come true. I have always loved you, Anne, more than you could ever know."

I kissed her and the tiny room filled with smiles and polite applause.

I didn't know it at the time, but Anne had already run *the* idea past JR before she and I spent that magical night at Berns. We drove up to Gainesville about two weeks later for one of our many visits with him.

When I first saw him, he threw his arms around me and said, "Mom and I both love you, Uncle Mike. I could not have gotten more awesome news. I am so stoked that neither of you will be alone any more."

He was *stoked*. A person couldn't get a better review.

He had told me in three short sentences all I wanted to know—that I was still Uncle Mike, not "dad," and seeing his mother and me so happy was something that he genuinely cared about. In many ways, nothing much had changed for him, which only added to the depth of our joy.

TWENTY-NINE

During that first year, I made so many excuses to be in Tampa it began testing my creativity. Anne and I were so happy whenever we could be together, most often just the two of us, hanging out. We did simple things like having drinks on the beach at Pass-a-Grille to toast another sunset, visiting local flea markets, or enjoying T-shirt and jean dinners in Ybor City, Tampa's very authentic Cuban section. Just spending time together was our favorite thing to do. Finally, I couldn't stand any more time apart from her. I accepted a sports writing position at the *St. Petersburg Times*. Eventually, Anne and I moved into a beautiful condo on Tierra Verde near St. Pete Beach. I even bought a boat.

It didn't take either of us long to decide on making our relationship official. Anne showed me a secluded and peaceful spot that she used to visit often during the years following Billy's death. It was a place where the earth, the sky, and the sea met every morning at first light. She said she felt closest to him there.

About a million years ago, the Gulf of Mexico took a huge bite out of the western Florida coastline and created what we now know as Tampa Bay. On the northern shore, where the Gulf merges its waters with the Bay, sits Fort DeSoto, a state park. Its bleached white beach extends for miles around the edges where the preserve touches the water. Although the area welcomes visitors every day, there are still long stretches of sand that are left alone to only the gulls and the ocean breezes.

We planned a casual wedding there. Surrounded by a few close friends, JR, and Billy's memory, we stood in ankle deep surf and exchanged simple, handwritten vows. We did it at sunrise to signify a new beginning for each of us. It had taken almost twenty years to reach that magnificent, earthy place. It took only minutes to pledge the rest of our time to each other. The moment, for me, was breathtaking.

Our new life was more wonderful than I could ever describe. I would often pinch myself. Still do.

During our trips to see JR, small talk about school and campus life usually melted rather quickly into golf talk. On one visit, JR asked if I had seen the latest news: Inverness had been granted another U.S. Open, filling in for an eastern club that was forced to withdraw from its place in the rotation. The Open would be back at Inverness only two years after he graduated from the University of Florida.

JR was excited. "How cool would it be, Uncle Mike, for me to qualify for *that* Open? I should be a professional for at least a year before then. That should be enough time to get ready, don't you think?"

I said with considerable enthusiasm, "I think that is a tremendous goal to set for yourself, JR. I'll bet that Inverness would love to see another Thompson on their leader board." I knew what he was thinking.

THIRTY

Although JR and I would discuss the looming Open at Inverness many times, the months and years between that first innocent conversation and the qualifying tournament for the Inverness Open seemed to fly by. It included several milestones.

The first, of course, was graduation, a glorious day for Anne and me. Adam, along with Tim and Ruth Fennell, joined us to make it all the more special. JR graduated with honors, something that made us all very proud. By now, he stood 6' 3" and weighed nearly 210 pounds. He had his mother's blonde hair and his dad's dark blue eyes. More striking than his handsome countenance, however, was something that shown brightly from the inside out. He had their character.

JR turned professional the next day. He and Johnny knocked around a number of mini-tours throughout the summer, all geared toward preparing for Q-school in October, the finals of which would be in Fort Worth, at Colonial Country Club. We always knew where he was, what he was doing. Every week we would get at least two phone calls providing the latest news. He never let us forget how much his family meant to him.

In September, JR made it through the first two stages to reach the finals of Q-School, although each advancement was more difficult because of his balky putter. In Fort Worth, he really struggled. The weather was unstable, cold and rainy for nearly the entire six-round event. JR's ball striking was solid but not as sharp as we had become accustomed to. His putting, however, was simply miserable. He finished 50th, which put him solidly on the Nationwide Tour. His anticipated PGA Tour career would have to wait.

It was right around that time that Anne received a letter from Spider Monroe. It was obviously written with hands filled with arthritis, and a heart full of memories and admiration.

Dear Miss Anne:

I am sure, by now, Mr. Howe has told you that I can no longer walk. He has been so charitable in finding me a nice place to live here in Newburgh. The food is good and the people are kind to me.

I hope this note finds you and young Mr. Billy in good health and spirit. Mr. Mike has called me regularly and I have been grateful to learn all I can about your new life and your son's golf. I understand that he is following in his daddy's footprints. God bless him for that.

Mr. Billy was the finest man I ever knew and I often take great comfort in my memories of him and the times we shared. I have always been most proud of our friendship. Like you and Mr. Mike, I miss him terribly.

During our cold, final round together, Mr. Billy gave me his player's badge to remind me of the worst day we would ever spend on a golf course. He was wrong.

As it turned out, for me, it was the very best day, and the badge has reminded me of it ever since.

I thought it would be most fitting for your son to have it from now on.

With fondest regards,
Spider Monroe

Out of the envelope fell the tarnished badge from the Inverness Open. It has adorned JR's golf bag ever since. He touches it before every round he plays.

Only a month or so had gone by after Spider's letter arrived when Ralph Howe called to inform us that Spider had peacefully passed away in his sleep. Once again, another great and gentle soul had been called home.

As it turned out, the year that JR spent on the Nationwide Tour was probably the best thing that could have happened to him. He and Johnny learned more about traveling together and their friendship grew ever stronger. Johnny's wild sense of humor always kept JR from becoming too intense and his stories helped strengthen their bond.

One day during a long drive to the next event, Johnny announced that he had been giving lessons at Bloomingdale whenever they were home for a week or so. The members loved seeing him and Tim Fennell encouraged some of them to work with Johnny. He had actually become quite a good teacher of golf's fundamentals, but he always made light of his teaching talent.

"You wanna know how good a teacher I am, JR?" Johnny asked, turning down the radio as their car roared down the highway.

"You remember Bobby Swanson's mother?"

"Sure," smiled JR, "Short and a little on the round side." He knew a story was coming.

"Yeah, that's her. Well she came to me a couple of months ago and complained that when she swung at the ball, it would often hit her in the left ankle. I said to myself, this I gotta see. So I teed up a ball on the range and jumped back quick 'cause she was on 'go.' She takes a healthy cut at this thing; the ball ricochets off the *inside* of the hosel and whacks her in the ankle again. Now she's doing the jig and even though I'm feelin' sorry for her pain, I'm trying hard not to fall on the ground laughin'."

He paused for JR to catch his breath. "Now, you wanna know how good a teacher I am JR? Huh? In only three weeks, I got her shankin' it *the other way.*"

Johnny was watching JR's reaction, which was convulsive laughter. He knew his stories always cracked JR up, and of course, that just encouraged him to make a new comedy routine out of virtually everything he did.

"Remember Mr. Randolph, JR?"

"Old Mr. Randolph?" JR asked, his chest still heaving. "Jeez, how old is that guy?"

"'Bout two years older than baseball, I think. Anyhow, what's up with old guys? Every time they talk to you they're in the middle of eating something and they've always gotta stand real close. And it's usually tuna salad, egg salad, chicken salad. With every hard 't' or 's,' the chunks are flying all over the place."

JR was bracing himself all over again.

"Last week, Mr. Randolph comes up to me on the range, and of course, he's eating a chicken salad sandwich. He says,

'Hey, Johnny, how 'bout the *two* of us havin' lunch *to*gether *s*omeday?' I told him, 'That'd be great Mr. Randolph, if I had two pieces of toast I could eat my *shirt*.'"

JR was choking, "Jeez, Johnny, why do you always have to tell these stories when we're going 80 miles an hour? You're gonna get us killed." Tears were still streaming down JR's face. He glanced at Johnny, who was smiling back, obviously pleased with himself.

The tour was a grind to be sure, especially when they were gone for weeks at a time. But being together made it easier to endure, and their solid friendship and common goals made the journey exciting. And Johnny's humor kept each day fresh.

Unfortunately, JR's putting never measured up to the standards that the rest of his game set, and consequently, he was not high on the nationwide money list as the qualifier for the Open drew near.

The day finally came. I've never seen anyone so focused, so dedicated to a single mission. Even Johnny was deadly serious. JR easily made it through local qualifying.

His putting was still suspect at the regional the following week in Orlando, but a back nine surge with laser-like iron shots seeking every pin pulled him through. There were six spots being contested in Orlando. JR got the very last one with a tap-in birdie at the final green, set up by a blistering three-iron shot to within inches of the hole.

Stage one in his Open quest was complete. He had barely qualified, but he was *in*. Soon, he would return to the site of his father's triumphant three days, and ultimate tragedy.

THIRTY-ONE

THE UNITED STATES OPEN CHAMPIONSHIP INVERNESS CLUB TOLEDO, OHIO

I called a few old friends and arranged for private housing near the club for JR and Johnny. Anne and I would stay nearby with an old fraternity brother of mine. Toledo was home. I knew the territory pretty well.

Prior to the trip, Fennell spent an extraordinary amount of time with JR at Bloomingdale, preparing. He had asked the superintendent to double cut and roll a rear section of the large practice green and water the area only enough to keep it alive in the blistering Tampa afternoons of June. Tim wanted the green as fast as he could make it, one as firm as he was sure JR would face under U.S. Open conditions. They worked long, exhausting hours on his putting and chipping.

Tim pulled me aside just before we left for Toledo.

"I'm really puzzled, Mike. JR's grip and stroke are as perfect as any I have ever seen. But I've never known a player of his caliber who consistently hits the lip of the hole, mostly the right lip. The putts look great, but nothing seems to drop. I don't know if I can help him. I think it might be his eyes."

125

Fennell looked worried. Human eyes are built for binocular vision, looking straight forward. But when a golfer is addressing a putt, he can only perceive the line with his sideways vision. Often what he sees from that position is not necessarily the correct line, and his target is not always where he is aimed. Consequently, even the best strokes produce perfect putts that are simply started off line and doomed from the beginning. Consistently hitting the lip of a hole only 4½ inches in diameter is a razorblade away from perfection and it can be maddening.

Fennell repeated dejectedly, "I think it might be his eyes."

The next day, I called David Graf, Head PGA Professional at Inverness, to get his advice. I knew Dave from his days on the golf team at the University of Toledo and I had heard from several sources that he was a marvelous teacher. He suggested that we bring JR in a few days early and he'd take a look.

When we arrived, Dave and JR headed directly for the practice green at Inverness. Newly resurfaced with G-2 bentgrass, it was like putting on a plate glass window.

After a few minutes, Dave walked over to me and said, "This kid's stroke and mechanics are perfect. It *has* to be his eyes. Let's go back to the shop. I've got a foolproof device that should tell us what we need to know."

It was a simple magnetic laser mechanism that attached to the face of JR's putter. David then asked JR to aim at a simulated "cup" at the far end of the room, a 4½-inch black dot painted on the floor. When JR felt he was dead on line, Dave flipped the switch on the laser. Sure enough, it was pointing considerably to the right. Dave explained that JR didn't have the time to re-train his eyes for the Open. He would have to simply aim farther left than he thought necessary on every putt. It would not be the perfect fix, not by a long shot, but it should give him a better chance to hole an extra putt or two. A few more putts dropped might well put JR in contention.

As soon as Adam registered, he began looking for JR. He found him in front of Billy's glass case at the end of the locker room. They hugged like brothers. Adam tried to ignore the tears streaming down JR's cheeks, gently patting his young friend on the back. They stood there together for several minutes in silence.

Finally, King suggested that he and JR play all their practice rounds together, an opportunity that many regular players on Tour would have killed for. JR was thrilled.

Each day, they played early to beat the heat and to avoid the afternoon crush of autograph hungry fans. It wasn't as though Adam didn't want to sign autographs. He knew that came with the territory. It was just the reality anymore for him that, once he started, it could take a very long time, or the appearance of rudeness, to break away. He was focused on preparation for the Open and wanted the least amount of distraction possible.

"I didn't realize that this was the place your dad set on fire years ago," Adam said to JR as they walked up the first fairway of their last practice day together. "I can't imagine how horrible that must have been for your mother. What a terrible thing to happen to anyone, let alone a player with the U.S. Open in the palm of his hand."

"Yeah," JR replied. "My Uncle Mike has told me about that whole week many times. Even though I was only three at the time, all the stories have made me feel as if I had seen it all firsthand. Everyone says he was a wonderful dad, that he deeply loved my mother, and was a great guy. Those are the parts of the story that I like hearing about the most. Those are the stories that make him real for me."

They walked several yards down the fairway. JR then added, "I don't mind telling you, Adam. What happened to my dad just wasn't right. Someday, I intend to win this championship for him."

Adam put his hand on JR's shoulder. "I hope you do, kid, I really do. But, make sure it's not at my expense, OK?" They both laughed and played on.

But King had an eerie feeling. If anyone was going to knock him off the throne, JR just might someday be the one good enough to do it.

THIRTY-TWO

Thursday's first round began at 7:30 A.M., a little chilly, with long shadows stretching across the course from the east. I didn't think it was anything more than coincidence when JR drew the same starting time as Billy had two decades earlier, *7:45 A.M.*

At this time of the day, galleries were thin. Early arrivals scouted out their favorite vantage points, mostly in the grandstands. They would settle there all day to watch a parade of players pass through a particular part of the course.

Behind the third green, a treacherous par-3 with water at greenside right, was a popular spot to catch the early action. JR's third group included a club pro from Kansas and an extremely nervous amateur from Pittsburgh. They had both shown the water too much respect and found the left side bunker with their tee shots.

JR's tee shot from 205 yards was a rope, a solid four-iron directly at the rear left hole location. The ball landed about 15 feet in front of the hole, took two hard bounces trying to dig into the ultra firm surface and *hit the pin.* The first mini-roar of the day went up as his ball spun to about six feet away. After the others had played onto the green, JR lined up what he hoped would be the first birdie of his first U.S. Open. But just like all the hours at Bloomingdale, his ball caught the right lip of the cup and stopped just behind the hole.

That effortless, but disappointing, par was to become a microcosm of his overall first round performance. JR finished at 71, even par, and very respectable. He hit an astounding *sixteen* greens in regulation figures, a phenomenal performance. However, his miserable total of 34 putts left many opportunities, like the one at the third, unfulfilled.

The first round ended, almost at sundown. A veteran club professional from Los Angeles held the lead with a brilliant 66. Lurking a shot behind was Adam King.

THIRTY-THREE

By the time JR and Johnny had begun their warm-up the following afternoon, the lead had gone from 5 under par to 8. The huge scoreboard behind the clubhouse was a sea of red figures, signifying under par scores. They were becoming commonplace. Seizing command were the touring pros, big names and journeymen alike, all taking turns at the lead. Birdies, and an occasional eagle, were being racked up all over the course and several large galleries sent regular, overlapping cheers from every corner of the property.

"Man, it sounds like everybody's takin' it deep today, JR," Johnny said, a little tinge of concern in his voice.

"Yeah, I know," JR replied. They wouldn't tee off for another hour, just after 3 P.M. 'Imagine what the lead could be by then,' he thought to himself. "We just have to keep focused on what *we* can control, Johnny," JR reminded him.

His warm-up had gone very well and on the practice green, just before being called to the tee, something clicked.

Golfers are by nature, fiddlers. For no conscious reason, JR had opened his stance slightly on a few short putts. They had all gone in with authority and he felt he could see the line much better from that position. He quietly mentioned it to Johnny and Johnny replied with a toothy grin, "Hey, let's go with it."

From tee to green, JR's round was even more surgical than the day before. His ball striking was solid and effortless, as always, but his distance control was downright magnificent. He and Johnny always seemed to pull the right club, hit the right shot, and gauge the wind perfectly.

But, unlike his first round, JR started cashing in on those shots that got in close enough to be termed "green light specials," putts that a pro knows he can take a run at without much jeopardy of having it run away and threaten a three-putt green. JR birdied four holes, *on each nine*. Coupled with a lone bogey at the seventh, his late-day posting of 7 under par-64 brought him to within three shots of the lead.

At 10 under par, the leader was a familiar name—*Adam King*.

THIRTY-FOUR

I'm not much of a believer in *deja vu*, but the damnedest thing happened the night before the third round. A cold front, much like the one that Billy had to contend with so long ago, charged across Lake Michigan from northwestern Canada. Temperatures were predicted to drop nearly 40 degrees overnight, from near 90 to somewhere in the 50s, with lots of wind. Although extremely rare for northwestern Ohio in June, it was now happening again to a Thompson I loved.

JR and I were watching the weather forecast that night. It wasn't what your average Florida boy wanted to hear, let alone experience, I can assure you. He turned away from the television, and asked, "Uncle Mike, isn't this the same kind of thing that happened to Dad?"

"It sure is," I complained. "I can't believe it, JR." The despair in my voice was much too obvious. "You and Johnny, a couple of Florida boys, aren't prepared for something like this. It's going to be miserable." I knew I looked dejected.

"Well, how did Dad handle it, Uncle Mike?" JR asked, upbeat and already knowing the answer.

Johnny piped in, "Probably the same way we did in Columbus two years ago when we played in the Buckeye Invitational at Ohio State. Remember? It snowed, *sideways.*"

He was standing now. "Is there a sporting goods store nearby, Mike?" Johnny asked. "All we need are some of those hand warmer bags that you shake, some winter gloves and a couple of wool hats. We've got the rest, weatherproof rain gear, waterproof shoes, cashmere sweaters. And we know how to 'layer' just like JR's dad did." Johnny was excited now. "I've heard those stories too, you know."

Even before sunrise, the wind was howling, sending an ominous, moaning chant through the trees. It would be the coldest for the fellows with the earlier tee times. As it turned out, none would play well. They had *lots* of company. Several early scores were in the high 70s and well into the 80s. Par on that day didn't relate to anything printed on the scorecard.

Although it didn't rain much, the wind was wicked, often blowing solid shots 25 yards off line. Standing still over a putt was virtually impossible. The whole day was brutal, for everyone.

JR was in the fourth group from the last. The course, which saw over 35,000 people the day before, was practically deserted. Television announcers and camera operators had a particularly difficult time sitting stationary with no way to stay warm. Extra rigging had been installed to keep their fragile perches upright and somewhat steady. Many pros who got over par early either stopped caring or withdrew altogether.

JR was lucky. He was prepared. His wonderful ball-striking could keep a ball low into the wind, or he could spin a shot enough to hold it against a side wind. Even with all his tee-to-green skills and his Florida ability to play in the wind, he remembered what Fennell used to preach about playing in heavy gusts.

"The key on a day like this one," Tim would repeat, "was the quality of a man's short game."

All those hours at Bloomingdale around the short game area were about to pay off.

JR played four of the opening six holes downwind, with one bogey. The two par-3s had heavy wind, left to right, and he hit low, hard hooks into each green. The shots were not pretty but very effective, producing pars. At the long par-4 seventh, the course turned hard into a howling northwest gale, which was ripping through the trees when JR and Johnny reached the tee. The light rain, now horizontal, stung their faces.

On the two previous days, JR had negotiated the 481 yards with a smoking drive and a solid six-iron second. However, on that day, *no one* in the field could reach the green in two shots. Like a veteran, he accepted what the wind would give him. He played his tee shot down the left side of the hole to avoid the creek, and his second, a three-metal, hooked low into the steep bank below the green. From there, JR played a brilliant low flying pitch up the slope that landed short of the hole, bounced once and checked hard only two feet below the cup for an easy, uphill putt. He had played the *exact* three shots that he had envisioned from the tee, the only three shots that could produce the par he wanted. It was one of many examples on this horrible day of JR's brilliant shot selection, execution, and course management. Fennell was right. JR was definitely a thoroughbred.

He fought hard all day, lost some of the battles, but definitely won the war. His one over par-72 was the low round of the day and one of the greatest, most demanding rounds of pure golf I had ever seen.

Adam played brilliantly as well. His 75 was one of only three scores of 75 or better in the third round. However, his round dropped his total back to 6 under par, *now tying him with JR for the lead.* No one else was under par for the tournament, no one even close. JR and Adam were out in front, alone. They would be paired together as the final twosome of the U.S. Open.

THIRTY-FIVE

Just as quickly as it moved in, the front disappeared by midnight. The morning of the fourth round dawned bright, cloudless, and still.

JR's arrival at the club was considerably different from the other arrivals of his young career. With each day's climb up the leader board, JR became less and less of an anonymous journeyman. Now he was tied for the lead in the final round of the U.S. Open with Adam King, his old friend and golf's perennial superstar.

By now, the story of his father's tragedy here a quarter century ago, and JR's subsequent quest to avenge it, was known by virtually every fan of the game. He had become a folk hero to thousands of them and the darling of sports writers who, just a week before, could not have picked him out of a police lineup.

The public contrast between the two was startling. It was David and Goliath in soft spikes. Even a few of Adam's staunchest supporters were openly pulling for JR to complete one of the most improbable stories in sports history. Most agreed, it was a mismatch. Many fervently wished, but few thought it possible.

JR refused a courtesy driver all week, choosing to drive to the club himself. During each short trip, he was particularly vigilant, but on *this* morning, downright cautious.

Pulling to a stop in the player's lot, he felt a strange sadness come over him. He sat motionless for a moment, reflecting. In having simply *arrived*, he had just accomplished something his father had been unable to do. His last thought was, 'This is the round you never got to play, Dad, and this is the one round I've been waiting my entire life to play. Every step, every shot...this one's for you. I'm going to try my very best...watch over me.'

He stepped from the car.

Several reporters and hundreds of new fans were clamoring for a sound bite or an autograph. He remembered the note that Adam had placed in his locker the night before. It was congratulatory and sincere. It ended, "Tomorrow, be courteous, even friendly, *but always, keep moving.*"

The note was thoughtful and even though they would do battle today, his kindness remained consistent. Both knew that their friendship would survive regardless of the day's outcome. Each was a consummate competitor and each wanted the best effort from the other. The note made him feel good, which was Adam's intention. Signing autographs and simultaneously answering reporter's questions, JR continued at a steady pace toward the clubhouse. It was very good advice.

Inside the quiet locker room, JR's oak locker had more notes from well-wishers. He read a few and decided to save the rest for later. Attendants, club members assigned to locker room duty for the tournament, and USGA officials all stopped briefly to wish him well. JR felt a powerful rush knowing so many people were pulling for him, but the butterflies were already lining up on the runway. He knew being nervous was normal for someone in this kind of uncharted water. He also thought it was a good sign. His body was getting ready. He felt strong and loose, and couldn't wait to begin the most important warm-up routine of his life.

Before leaving, he stopped, alone, in front of Billy's display, slowly read the inscription again, and momentarily put his hand on the glass. "Today, Dad," he whispered softly, "you'll get every last ounce of what I have to give."

There were no tears now, only steely resolve.

Johnny was already waiting for him at the practice tee. Not able to sleep, he nervously arrived just after sunrise and had already walked the course. He made careful notes of all the hole locations, especially those toward the end of the round when a truly courageous shot might be called for.

Johnny was wearing the crisp white jumpsuit required of all caddies in the Open. Even though the temperature already approached 90 degrees, Johnny turned up his collar to protect his vulnerable Irish, freckled skin. Protruding from the sides and back of his white cap was a frizzy shock of red hair that begged for a barber. On this most important day of his caddy career, however, Johnny did not feel well. He passed it off as nerves, the heat, not enough sleep. 'Whatever,' he thought, 'it'll pass.'

JR walked onto the range. "Morning, pards," he said to Johnny, "got anything goin' on this fine morning?"

"Nothin' much," said Johnny, "just fixin' to tote for the new Open champion is all."

JR smiled, stretched a bit, and began his routine, swinging two clubs rather slowly. The first ten balls or so were short pitches with his sand wedge, just for rhythm. He gradually made his way up through the set, always aiming at an appropriately distanced target. He worked each club—practicing fades, left to right, then right to left draws—all landing on target. Every divot was dollar sized, thin, each one peeled next to the last, forming an almost perfect rectangle of disturbed turf when he was finished. Ball-striking for JR had always been effortless. His shots were so solid, they even sounded different from many of the other pros.

After all their time together, JR's fluid swing continued to completely amaze Johnny with the finesse and power it produced. For Johnny, now a 10 handicapper at best, the practice tee with JR was always one of his favorite places. From their humble beginnings, he silently reveled in being a part of something destined to be very special.

Somewhere in the middle of their practice session, Adam arrived. He settled in at the far end of the practice tee. JR glanced over his shoulder. He and King exchanged nods and smiles before returning to the work at hand.

Finally, JR had the driver in his hands, sending rockets to the far end of the range, an exhibition that dropped jaws in the gallery. Considering the brutally deep U.S. Open rough throughout the course, this could become the most important club in his bag today. He had driven it beautifully throughout the tournament so he was rightly more concerned with how well his balky putter would behave.

As he and Johnny prepared to leave for extra work on the putting green, JR finally noticed how pale Johnny's face had become, the perspiration, the fog in his eyes.

"Are you OK, Johnny?"

"Yah, I'll be fine, boss. Don't worry 'bout me." Johnny struggled to mask how he was really feeling. He would simply "tough it out," he thought. After all, JR didn't need any further distractions.

Before leaving, JR signed a few more autographs for the members who had been assigned to range duty throughout the week. They all wished him well. His genuine personality had made them all feel like old friends.

THIRTY-SIX

A large gallery had formed around the putting green at Inverness, straining to get a close look at the leaders.

JR stepped through the ropes amidst the crowd's courteous murmur. They all marveled at the pro's deft touch, especially on surfaces that seemed as slick as marble. Quiet and respectful, they watched JR line up six balls, each about three feet farther from the hole. Working from the closest ball first, JR would line up each putt with his eyes on the hole, allowing his brain to compute the distance. One final look at the ball and release. His father had written about the drill in an early issue of *Golf* magazine. A tattered copy of that article was always in JR's golf bag, more of a connection than a reminder. That routine began his every putting session. Today, it felt good. His stroke was slow, smooth, and rhythmic. Ball after ball found the cup. Twenty minutes to tee time.

JR was ready, like a racehorse nearing the gate.

One final check, like always, before leaving for the first tee. Both he and Johnny counted the clubs, fourteen. Golf balls, all Titleist 1s, marked with a black dot over the middle "t." Three long tees. Three Canadian dimes for markers. New glove, broken in on the range. Yardage book along with Johnny's pin locations and notes. The time had come.

In these last few minutes before the start of the final round, JR visualized his first tee shot of the day. He felt it was critical to start any round on a positive note. Today, he would aim at the last fairway bunker on the left and hit a faded three-metal to the middle of the fairway. Setting the tone on today's first tee shot would be huge.

Then…the unbelievable happened.

JR heard a chilling, moaning sound. It came from Johnny. JR turned and watched his friend crumple to the ground.

"Johnny, what's wrong?"

Johnny's face was now pale and covered in beads of sweat. He shuddered in wrenching pain. He looked at JR, eyes squinting and grabbing his right side.

"I can't breathe, JR. It hurts so bad." Breathless, he added, "Go without me, I'll catch up."

But JR knew immediately that "catching up" would not happen today. His brain raced, his heart pounded. 'I can't leave my friend,' he thought.

Greenside officials immediately called for medical assistance, then radioed the starters. Staff doctors surrounded Johnny and swiftly diagnosed his condition as appendicitis. They placed him on a stretcher and moved him to a nearby ambulance. The doctors assured JR that Johnny was safe and since there was nothing further he could do for his friend, he should go…*go now.*

Johnny braved a smile and flashed a weak "thumbs up."

Shaken to the core, JR picked up his golf bag and began hurrying toward the first tee. Tournament officials and police officers parted the crowd, escorting JR. Halfway there, a disheveled old man stepped from under the ropes and offered to help JR with his clubs. One of the officials tried to push him back.

"You ever caddied before?" JR said, nearly out of breath.

Still being pushed backward, the old man responded, "Yes sir, you bet." The crowd jostled them even more.

"You any good?" asked JR, as he stepped between the official and the old man. They came face to face.

"I'm damned good," came the instant reply.

JR looked past the three-day-old stubble and into the clearest set of blue eyes he had ever seen.

"You'd better be," he said, and helped him wrestle the large tour bag to his shoulder. JR slipped his three-metal from the bag and handed the headcover to the old man as they hustled toward the first tee. "'Cause you're all I've got."

THIRTY-SEVEN

Still rattled and with his focus shattered by the last few minutes, JR reached the tee. The starters and Adam were waiting.

King stepped forward. "Look," he said, "take as much time as you need. I've cleared it with the starter. We're not really that far behind. No sweat."

"Thanks, man." JR breathed heavily as they patted each other on the back.

Although the rules call for a 2-shot penalty for arriving late for a scheduled tee time, the bizarre circumstances prevented any such consideration. They shook hands, identified their golf balls and wished each other luck.

Adam came close to JR's ear, hand on his shoulder.

"Eyes forward, my friend. One shot at a time. I'm sure Johnny will be fine." His hand squeezed JR's shoulder a little stronger. "Play well," he said.

"Thanks, Adam." Their eyes met. "Thanks again."

Everything settled into silence.

The starter's booming voice announced, "Ladies and gentlemen, this is today's final pairing. On the tee, from Orlando, Florida, the reigning United States Open Champion, with a three-round total of 6 under par...*Adam King.*"

Amidst loud and enthusiastic applause, King touched the bill of his cap, mouthed the words "thank you," took a deep breath and stepped forward to address his tee shot. King was a lithe, athletic man with immense power. Since his days with JR at Bloomingdale, his new training regimen had added twenty pounds of pure muscle. Like JR, he chose a three-metal and to the gallery's delight, his crackling first shot of the final round split the fairway.

Following JR's wishes from the start of the tournament, the starter introduced him to the large and excited crowd. From his first word, they drew silent.

"Now on the tee, from Valrico, Florida, tied for the lead at 6 under par...*Billy Thompson, Junior.*"

The gallery erupted for several seconds before JR held up his hand. Respectful silence fell across the tee. JR's concern for Johnny, and the ensuing confusion, had kept his mind off this critical first shot. Now, there was no time for nervous tension to build. In seconds, he was standing over it.

Focus, concentration, and years of preparation took over. JR's long, fluid swing produced a missile, directly on line with the last fairway bunker on the left before beginning a slow fade back into the safety of the short grass. Holding his wonderfully balanced finish, he spun the club in his hands. He had hit a beauty.

The crowd roared as both players left the tee in a brisk, determined pace, not acknowledging each other.

The gladiators were away. *The game was on.*

THIRTY-EIGHT

"I suppose if we're going to spend this pleasant afternoon together, I should probably know your name." JR said, looking to the much shorter and older man keeping pace at his side, the clubs clinking in rhythm with each step.

"My friends all call me 'Doc,'" he said, "have for a long time."

"Really?" JR was surprised. "What branch of medicine?" he asked, still taking long strides toward the Titleist 1 in the fairway, several yards ahead.

"Oh," chuckled the old man, "I'm no doctor. Not near smart enough, that's for sure. Some years ago, though, I played a little golf for money. I was pretty good, I guess, with the flat stick, especially long putts. One day, after a particularly long one went in for all the cash, one of the boys said in painful disgust, '*Doctor Draino, makin' another house call.*'"

He looked at JR with a twinkle in his eye as they reached the ball. "It's been 'Doc' ever since."

"So you were a pro, too." JR said.

The old man slightly shrugged his shoulders. "That was a very long time ago, Mr. Thompson but, yes sir...yes I was."

"Good," JR's voice was now deadly serious, "then you have some idea of what we're up against." The old pro solemnly nodded.

JR's voice turned friendly again. "And my name's JR, OK, Doc?" Another smile from the old pro, and the introductions were over. Time for business.

King's nine-iron second shot had spun back to within eight feet below the hole, a perfect position for an opening birdie, which he would eventually convert. JR's second, a soaring nine-iron of his own, landed beyond the hole and stayed there. He two-putted for a par and was one stroke down after the opening hole.

The second and third holes, a par-4 and a treacherous par-3, were both halved in pars. JR had two good chances for birdies, having hit each of his approaches well inside those of King, but his putter reverted to its old ways. Both putts had good speed, each catching the cup's edge. The worst kind of putting, really. Good enough to be *so* close to perfect and yet no reward. It wears on a player over time.

The brutal par-4 fourth, a former par-5 in earlier Opens, was the beginning of a stretch of extremely difficult holes dubbed by the members as "*broken jaw corner.*" Each hole had the potential of throwing the ultimate, and early, knockout punch. Every player paid extra close attention through this stretch. They were always happy to reach the eighth tee without doing too much damage.

In spite of a slight head wind, both King and JR had driven their tee shots long and straight to the crest of a fairway ridge, leaving about 180 yards to the pin. The hole was located in the diabolical right front quarter, an extremely difficult section of the green bordered on all sides by severe slopes. King again went first. His second, a five-iron, was dead on line, just past the hole. It held within 20 feet, a remarkable shot.

JR, too, took dead aim. Beautifully played, his second was also directly at the flag. But, during its flight, a slight increase in the breeze was just enough to prevent its full carry. It was only a matter of a few feet, but the shot landed slightly short of the hole, hesitated, and began rolling slowly at first and then gathered pace as it rolled off the front of the green and halfway down the steep hill fronting the greensite.

JR's pitch up the hill stopped about four feet to the left of the hole, remarkable from where he was. But when King's putt, to a thunderous roar, dropped for a rare fourth-hole birdie, and JR's par putt, once again, lipped the cup, he found himself quickly three shots behind. Like many band-aids in golf, his putting adjustment from two days ago was no longer working.

The sight from the par-4 fifth tee is like looking down a rather large funnel. Several trees and a severe ridge on the left, coupled with a creek edging in from the right, made the landing area narrower and narrower the farther one ventured down the fairway. The safe shot from the tee was with a three-metal to a spot where the fairway still had some width. Anything more aggressive would require a distinctly right-to-left ball flight to avoid the creek.

King had the honor. Flushed with confidence, he chose the driver. The shot was bold, up the right side. But it carried too far and after a few hard bounces, found the creek. JR had his first opening. The old pro already had the head cover off the three-metal and he covered the driver with most of his body. JR took the hint. His tee shot was shorter than King's, but found dead center.

The right side of the fifth green is fronted by a steep bank down to the same creek, and the flagstick was just beyond it. JR played a wonderful, towering fade with his seven-iron, starting the shot to the left of the hole and drifting it back. It was beautiful, spinning to within six feet. From where they stood, it looked even closer, a sure birdie. The large gallery that had waited for hours in the grandstand to the rear of the green let loose a tremendous roar. Its sound and energy rolled back and slammed into each of them.

Even before King took his penalty drop from the water, he could see the infamous "broken jaw" fist coming his way. To further compound his problem, the area in which he was required to take relief from the creek was surrounded by trees, leaving no realistic shot to the green. He was forced to play to the left of the green, toward one of the deep bunkers there, and hope that he could somehow make a bogey five and at least limit the damage.

The following shot ended exactly where he had imagined, in the first of two deep bunkers on the left side of the green. His long bunker shot would be mostly downhill and extremely fast. He would need to be aggressive enough to get the ball up quickly and out of the bunker, but have it land softly enough to stay on the putting surface. He calculated that he could hit a high lob wedge far enough to carry the lip of the bunker and still have plenty of spin to provide a few soft bounces before releasing down the hill. Somehow, he thought, if he could just get a putt from five or six feet, he had a chance of preserving some of his early advantage. He also figured that JR would make his short birdie putt. Losing only one, or possibly two, strokes of his lead seemed like the best he could hope for.

JR and the old pro were standing calmly at the edge of the green when King's fourth shot cleared the bunker. The ball landed only three or four feet onto the putting surface, checked hard and then began a slow roll down the slope.

"Wow." JR said, shaking his head slowly in admiration as both he and the old man watched the ball gather speed.

The gallery was now on their feet, emotions rising. King had dashed out of the bunker and was racing up the slope to the green, teeth clenched, sand wedge held like a sword. The ball was really moving, moving fast, when it struck the bottom of the flagstick and immediately disappeared into the hole for a miraculous par. The crowd was ecstatic. JR stared in disbelief. The gallery's roar was that of a passing freight train.

King himself had coached his young friend, "Always expect your opponent to hole every shot he looks at, because when it happens, it won't shock your focus." But this one was, indeed, shocking.

JR slowly replaced his ball as the gallery noise died down. He could still gain a stroke with this birdie putt, not a terribly difficult one at that, he thought. It read just outside the right edge, a slight leftward break. The ball started exactly as he had aimed and stayed there, missing just on the right lip of the cup.

Every bit of air went out of the gallery in a collective, slumping moan. The old pro closed his eyes momentarily, gritting his teeth. No advantage had been taken of JR's two magnificent shots. King's three-shot lead had miraculously escaped intact.

At the sixth, a long par-3 guarded by deep bunkers on the front left and along the right side, both players hit magnificent shots. With the hole location in the deep right side behind a wall of sand, each had hit his approach up the middle of the green, leaving makeable 15-foot birdie putts. King was slightly away and on nearly the same line as JR's ball. His stroke was long and smooth and his putt rolled, as if on glass, directly into the middle of the cup. He was now three under par and about to go four shots ahead.

His heroics at the fifth had been a huge turnaround and King's mountainous confidence showed with each move. JR's putt became even more critical. He *had* to make it just to hold King at bay. He took his time, reading the putt from both sides. JR had also paid very close attention to King's putt. Even though his eyes were reading a fair amount of break, King's had not wavered. It had gone dead straight.

The old pro could see indecision creeping into JR's body language. He wanted desperately to help him read the putt, but JR had not even made eye contact with him, choosing to go about his work alone. JR finally, and stubbornly, decided to ignore what King's ball had told him. It was his sixth straight putting mistake. The ball never broke and hung on the left lip. *Four down.*

Fear and indecision are golf's most notorious and efficient killers. These two villains have ruined more individual shots and opportunities than anything else in the game's storied history.

JR did not know fear, never had. But enough misses will make any man begin doubting his choices. Worse still, they could make him start guessing, a hopeless place to be under normal circumstances. Now, JR was on the receiving end of a double-barreled problem. He was facing the world's greatest player, flush with confidence. He was dueling a man who was used to winning, used to winning U.S. Opens. And King was in full flight.

At the same time, JR felt almost helpless to stem the tide, like a sentry standing guard, but out of ammunition. His long walk to the seventh tee was filled with worry and creeping desperation.

THIRTY-NINE

The incomparable golf course architect, Donald Ross, wrote in his memoirs that one of his favorite challenges was to create a truly great golf hole without the necessity of sand bunkers. The magnificently natural seventh at Inverness must have made Ross extremely proud.

The tee and the green are on opposing ridges, about 450 yards apart. The floodplain below contains a winding fairway bordered on the left by a covey of long grass mounds, and on the right by a creek, definitely in play, carving its way along the fairway's edge. Two fine shots are required to reach a severely sloping green that is one of the most difficult on the course to putt.

King negotiated the hole with an excellent drive and a solid five-iron to the green's midsection. From there, he easily two-putted for his par. However, JR's second was one of the most memorable shots of the championship to that point. His towering six-iron landed about 15 feet short of the flagstick and on second bounce checked to within inches of the hole. An easy tap-in birdie meant that JR had negotiated "broken jaw corner" in even par numbers, but had still lost three strokes in the process.

It was only a short walk to the tee at the par-5 eighth, but JR's first birdie finally put a little spring in his step.

To the delight of the roving gallery, both King and JR blasted tee shots in excess of 300 yards, clearing the deep fairway bunkers on the left and leaving a reasonable chance to reach the green in two shots. JR's birdie at the seventh had given him a bit of momentum and being first to play his second shot at the eighth was an advantage. He ripped a hybrid iron about 220 yards and threaded the small opening between two greenside bunkers. His ball finished slightly through the green on the back fringe only 20 feet from the pin. Now the pressure shifted to King. His response was stunning.

Having replaced one of his long irons prior to the round for a seven-metal to handle the long rough, King had the perfect club in his bag for the long, high shot that confronted him from a slightly downhill lie. The resulting moon shot cleared all the greenside bunkers guarding the tight hole location, splattering a huge ball mark into the green and finished only six feet behind the hole. He would later say that it was one of the greatest shots of his career. JR couldn't help giving King a congratulatory slap on the shoulder as both smiling players walked side by side to the green.

By now, the gallery, and their enthusiasm, was rapidly growing with each successive hole. No one else on the course was making any sort of a charge. It was clear that the outcome would be settled between these two and at this stage in the final round, King was the odds-on favorite for the title. What happened next would only add to that conclusion.

JR's putt from the fringe was not a terribly long one and if distance alone was the deciding factor, it was makeable. JR had always preferred to putt from just off the green, especially when the fringes were in such magnificent shape as the ones at Inverness. But, unluckily, an irrigation head lay directly between his ball and the correct line of the putt. It left him no choice. He would have to play a delicate little chip shot, barely flying to the green's edge. It was a shot that King himself had shown him a few years before at Bloomingdale. He would play the ball back in his stance, directly opposite his right toe. Then, using his pitching wedge and gripping the club like his putter, he would simply make a long, slow putting stroke and let the loft of the club gently lift the ball into the air.

His touch was wonderful and the ball began rolling as soon as it landed on the edge of the green. The gallery cheered it down to the hole. It rolled true, right to the center of the cup, but it stopped tantalizingly short, just on the lip. Nonetheless, a solid birdie four.

King lined up his six-footer. He calmly set up to it, took one flowing practice stroke and then drilled it for an *eagle*. A massive roar again rolled across the course, sending notice that this Open had just been grabbed by the throat. Everyone hearing the roar instinctively knew it had to be King.

The front nine ended with par-4s for each of them. King was *5 under par* and held a commanding four-stroke lead. He showed no signs of cracking. Furthermore, JR had shown no real indication of being able to catch him. His one under par-34 on the opening nine had been solid, but his only birdies had been tap-ins. Without the ability to hole plenty of putts in the remaining nine holes, he didn't seem to have much of a chance.

Most people felt it was over. As King had proven so many times in the past, he was not only the Tour's top player, he was also the best "closer" in golf.

FORTY

The group ahead had experienced considerable trouble on the ninth hole and was just leaving the tenth tee when JR and King arrived through a tunnel of spectators created by marshals on either side. JR, knowing there was a little time to kill, walked to the back of the tee, munching on a fresh apple.

Dave Graf approached and said in a low voice, "I sent one of my staff to the hospital to give us regular reports on Johnny's condition. The operation went smoothly, JR, no complications and although he's going to be sore for a few weeks, Johnny's going to be just fine. Thought you'd want an update."

JR was relieved. "Thanks, Dave, I really appreciate your kindness. Can you get a message back to him for me?" JR asked.

"Sure thing." Dave assured.

"Tell Johnny that it's no fun wrestling this alligator *alone.*" They both laughed.

"We'll tell him, JR. Best of luck back here," Dave wished, pointing to the last nine.

Still waiting for the group in front to clear, JR finally turned to the old man and said "Doc, we better figure out something real quick. We're running out of holes."

This was the first time he had engaged the old pro in anything resembling a conversation since their strolling introduction on the opening hole. More than anything, he was just relieving some of the tension.

Continuing to clean the clubheads, Doc looked up at JR and said softly, "Truth be told, son, he's probably too far in front. *But,* everything's gone his way so far. We still have nine holes, you know. I have a feeling when this is over, he's gonna know he's been in a real dogfight. A couple of quick 'birds' might bloody his nose a bit, if you know what I mean."

JR returned the look with a wry grin, "You're a lot tougher old crow than you look, Doc. It's nice knowing I'm not really alone in this scrap."

"Not by a long shot, no sir," came the swift reply.

Then, almost as an afterthought, the old pro added, "You might want to think about having me read a few putts for you, back here. If you don't mind me sayin' so, I don't think you're seein' things so good. It's gettin' late, you know."

JR's eyebrows lifted and he let that idea settle in for a moment.

"I guess I couldn't do any worse, could I?"

The old man just shrugged his shoulders.

Parallel to the first hole, the tenth is usually played conservatively off the tee as well. A three-metal to the top of the ridge provides a downhill view of the tiny tenth green, situated just beyond a little stream that runs through several holes on the back nine. King made this very play, beautifully. It would leave him with no more than a downhill pitching wedge.

JR, now at last discussing things with the old pro, was reminded of the back left hole location. Just about any safe layup off the tee would require a second shot over two deep greenside bunkers to that very small section of the green. They decided to take a driver down the right side of the hole, a shot that, if hit hard, could reach the flat ground below the ridge and leave a short pitch directly up the center of the green to the hole. Bunkers on the ridge and tall rough below were standing guard, but JR striped his tee shot into good position, in the short rough down on the flat, a mere 70 yards from the pin.

King slid over close to his caddy as they left the tee. He was sure he had played the correct shot, but commented to his caddy, "Let's stay on our toes, Jeff. I know this young man very well. He'll be comin' after us, so we have to keep turning the screw."

Back shot the caddy's reply, "Four shots clear with only nine to go, and *you* in the lead? I like *our* chances, Boss," as they climbed the steep hill to reach the tenth fairway.

King played a smart second, a lofted pitching wedge wide of the pin to the center of the green, leaving about 20 feet. JR's ball had found the edge of the rough, but his ball was sitting up nicely. His second shot was dead on line, but lacking enough backspin; it trickled to the back of the green, about 15 feet away. The large gallery on the hillside behind the green had a bird's eye view of the ensuing putts. King's was dead center, but agonizingly short, by just a fraction. "Oooooh!" moaned thousands of voices.

During King's effort, the old pro had been looking over JR's try. He knew instinctively that there was more break than appeared at first glance. He could feel it in his feet. He waited for JR to ask. But JR had continued studying the putt on his own.

Then, returning to his ball from behind the hole, he *finally* looked over at the old man and said, "What's up, Doc?" The crowd cracked up and so did the old man. A good deal of tension evaporated in a breeze of laughter.

"Give it at least six inches on the right," he said quietly, returning quickly to the task.

"*That much?*" JR asked, as he bent down for another look.

The old man leaned in close to JR's ear. "Trust me, son." Doc's voice was so confident, and yet so calming.

JR thought, 'what the hell,' and honored the suggestion. To everyone in the crowd, the putt seemed far too wide at the start, but it quickly darted to the left and buried itself into the back of the cup. The roar was deafening.

JR jumped about as high as he could when the putt went in. There was definitely some magic in this rumpled old man. As they climbed the hill to the eleventh tee, side by side, JR turned his head and took a hard look at him. His caddy's eyes were looking straight ahead and a broad smile filled his face. The large bag rested across his lower back, but seemed of no burden. JR had a most comforting thought flash through his mind. I guess I'm really *not* alone today.

The lead had shrunk to three. JR had skillfully made his birdie, but King was not remotely worried. He knew that JR would need to continue making birdies and there were only three short holes left before the backbreaking stretch of long par-4s to the finish. Besides, he planned to make a few more birdies himself. They would, no doubt, seal the deal no matter what JR had in store.

At the short par-4 eleventh, as well as the par-3 twelfth, both players made solid pars, after each had come close to birdies. They then stepped to the short, and reachable, par-5 thirteenth with Adam still holding a commanding three-shot lead.

Six holes remained.

FORTY-ONE

The landing area off the thirteenth tee is dominated by a natural nose in the middle of the fairway, pointing directly at the green and creating severe slopes on both sides. The fairway, below, narrows to a mere 10 yards, bordered left and right by some of the most punishing rough on the course. The safe tee shot, a lay up, would create a much longer second shot, one that would have difficulty finding the green on the distant ridge. A bolder play with a driver would need a little luck to avoid the rough that chokes the fairway farther down.

JR stayed aggressive. His ensuing blast carried the nose and ran true down the middle of the fairway to within 200 yards of the green. The fairway was only two or three steps wide where his ball came to rest. His lips were pursed as he handed the club to the old pro.

King took a deep breath. His driver, too, was ripped. It nearly hit JR's ball as it ran another five yards beyond.

JR was first to play. The hole was cut in the right rear of the green, perilously close to a large, deep bunker guarding the right side. What little wind remaining was behind him, and from the left. He chose the more lofted of the two hybrid clubs in his bag. The shot was high and slightly left of the pin. As it flew, it began a slow fade from left to right.

"Hang on." JR pleaded.

"Get down!" the old pro chimed in. But the shot stayed in the air just long enough to drift into the bunker. Worse yet, it plugged.

King seized the opening. His four-iron second was a bullet, directly into the middle of the green and rolled to a stop about 12 feet to the left of the hole. Surely, *now* King would finish off the young pro from Valrico. His easy birdie, and possibly an eagle three, would be more than anyone could overcome with so few holes remaining. King and his caddy could feel it too and their strides grew longer as they marched up the hill toward the green. King could now smell blood in the water and he loved closing in for the kill, even if it would be at JR's expense.

JR's heart sank when he saw the lie he had drawn in the sand. Even with a clean lie, getting his ball up and in for a birdie would have been nearly impossible. But *this* ball was so close to the lip and buried, *really* deep. 'I'd have to be Houdini just to get this one *on the green,*' he thought.

The old pro saw his man's emotions sag.

"Look," he said with amazing confidence, his index finger tapping JR's chest, "you get it on the green, and *I'll get it in the hole.*"

His challenge snapped JR out of his funk. Even still, JR wondered if the old man had any real idea of how tough getting this ball up and out of this pit was going to be. The lie would prevent any spin at all on the shot and keeping it from rolling completely off this slick, sloping green was the second part of the miracle he was being asked to perform.

However, the words '*I'll get it in the hole*' were so intriguing, he put his hand on the old man's shoulder and said, "OK, Doc, I can't wait to see you pull *this* one off."

JR dug his feet deep into the sand. Those in the gallery on his side of the green couldn't even see the ball and many were shaking their heads at his predicament. They were also feeling the letdown of knowing that JR's bid was probably about to end.

JR's mind flashed back to the practice bunker at Bloomingdale. Fennell was standing next to him now, having just mashed a practice ball deep into the sand with his heel.

"Contrary to what you may have heard about buried lies," he said then, "I want you to open the blade of that sand wedge, *wide open*. Now," he continued, "lift the club directly over your right shoulder, just as if we were splitting cord wood for the fireplace. From there, drive the club vertically, deep into the sand behind the ball, as hard as you can."

JR remembered how high the shot came out that day, maybe it would today as well. 'OK, Tim, let's chop some wood,' he thought.

The downswing was violent, driving the open clubhead into the sand behind the buried ball. Sand flew in every direction, but just as it had on that day long ago, up it popped. The ball didn't fly far, but *just* far enough, reaching the putting surface on the second bounce and then began trickling down the slope toward the front of the green. When it stopped, it was on the front fringe, at least 50 feet away from the cup. He had gotten it out, but now he lay three to King's two and King was so much closer.

JR emerged from the bunker to polite applause. He handed the sand-covered club to the old pro and said in mock challenge, "OK, Doc, your turn."

"No problem," came the swift and stunning reply, prompting a quizzical look from JR. The old man kept the putter in his hand and lead JR to the bottom of the green. He got down

on his haunches behind the ball, shading his eyes from a sun that was now falling in the western sky.

He turned to JR with total certainty. "This putt is severely uphill and not as fast as it looks. Here's the key. Our ball will have to enter the hole from *behind.*" He pointed to a spot beyond the hole and to the left. "Imagine the cup is *there,* JR, not where it actually is. If you make the imaginary putt, *you'll make the real one.*"

JR knew the odds were astronomical, but decided to humor the old man and do it his way. At that point, desperation offered nothing else to lose.

The ball was struck with authority. Up the hill it climbed, beginning a long, curving sweep to the right. Much too long, JR's subconscious was telling him. However, the same steep slope that swiftly took his ball to the front of the green moments ago now sapped its speed. The ball slowed to a near halt and began creeping back down the hill, closer, closer, until the hole reached out *and sipped it in.*

Everyone watching jumped into the air, screaming in delight and wonder. King and JR both stood completely still for several seconds in total shock. As JR finally approached the hole to retrieve his ball, King said to him, annoyed, "I'll give you another hundred balls and you can't even get *close.*"

"I know," said JR, still completely stunned himself.

The old man was busily raking the bunker, chuckling to himself.

For the first time all week, King was visibly shaken. Some time had elapsed since he had played his last shot and he had just witnessed the most miraculous birdie that, only minutes before, had looked like a bogey, or at best, a par. It was just enough to cloud his amazing focus.

His twelve-footer for eagle brushed the low side of the hole. King's tap-in birdie still maintained his three-shot lead, but it no longer had the value he had earlier assigned. The lead may not have changed, but momentum had *definitely* swung.

JR lifted his golf bag upright and waited for Doc to exit the bunker. "How did you know?" he whispered, still amazed.

"I told you, JR, I was always good on the long ones." His eyes twinkled, "I just *knew*."

They headed for number fourteen, still three behind, but pumped.

FORTY-TWO

Many athletes, in nearly every sport, have long been fascinated with "The Zone." It is a mystical place in the subconscious mind where performance is effortless, fear does not exist, mistakes don't happen, and every decision is the right one. It is a blissful state visited by only the lucky few, and then, only once or twice in an entire career.

No one knows how to get there. There are no roadmaps, no directions, no magical GPS systems to reach The Zone. No one can see it coming, not even the receiver. But, now and then, something totally unexpected happens, usually something quite dramatic. It is then that, mysteriously, the door to The Zone pops open, invisible to everyone else, and in steps the performer. Once inside, he is invincible.

Late in the afternoon of that U.S. Open's last round, JR saw the "door" pop open on the thirteenth green, and blissfully, amidst the raucous roaring of the crowd, he quietly stepped into...The Zone.

Now playing like a man possessed, he birdied the fearsome fourteenth and parred the long fifteenth, both by holing putts in excess of 20 feet, each read deftly by the old man. It did not seem to matter to JR that he had been matched by

King's own magic. He now stood on the sixteenth tee, *still three strokes behind,* but never feeling stronger or more confident in his entire life.

Both played wonderful, long tee shots, threaded between several fairway bunkers laying in wait. Thousands of people surrounded the hole, ten to twelve deep in most places, stretching and straining to catch a glimpse of the action. Everyone felt the unmistakable sense of witnessing history in the making.

The pin was, again, in a very difficult location, in the left front of the green, on a downslope. It would be best to putt from behind the hole, uphill to the cup.

JR and the old pro were in complete lockstep with one another, their thoughts and vision as one. The planned shot, a right-to-left draw with an eight-iron, came off as if lifted from a video replay, landed short and to the right of the flagstick before trickling down the slope, past the pin, leaving an uphill birdie attempt of only 10 feet. From several vantage points, thousands of eyes watched it land, roaring in unison.

King had virtually the same shot. He had just seen the blueprint and needed only to duplicate it. His shot, too, had some hook spin, bringing it in from the right. But he overcooked it slightly and his ball missed the green by only a foot or so, finishing in the left greenside bunker.

JR, now flying free in The Zone, was amazed at how clear his mind was, how sharp his focus. He knew the situation. The approaching moment was his to seize. Destiny was taking shape and he knew, as sure as his next breath, that he was *going to make* this putt in front of him. Everything about the moment was slowing down, a feeling that confirmed his thoughts.

King also saw the situation clearly. He would have to play a very delicate, risky shot to get close to the hole that was cut so close to his side of the green. He addressed the ball and began his slow, deliberate swing.

But his bunker shot lacked the familiar thump. *It was short. The ball failed to clear the lip.*

He had gotten a little too cute, shaving a little too much, in trying to lay his shot dead to the hole. The ball hit the bank of the bunker and rolled back to his feet. King stood there, looking at it in disbelief. The crowd gasped at first, then began murmuring, re-calculating JR's chances. King took little time on the second attempt. This time, an unmistakable *thuuump,* and his ball landed just short of the cup, checked hard, and lay dead only inches away.

The resulting bogey now handed JR his biggest opportunity of the day. The old man leaned in close to help read the putt. "Remember the bloody nose, JR? Let's land a haymaker on him, right now."

"Get the smelling salts ready, Doc," JR said with ice in his words. The stroke was smooth and confidant, the ball dead on-line. The gallery, frenzied, began running as soon as the ball disappeared. The lead had melted to *one.* Only two holes remained.

———

At 470 yards, the par-4 seventeenth at Inverness is a long, difficult dogleg left. With the length both players possessed, their tee shots had to be shaped, right-to-left, to avoid the bunkers and deep rough on the outside of the dogleg. Forming the inside of the elbow is the deepest, highest banked bunker on the entire course. No one could escape it using more than a sand wedge.

The distant, tilted green sits well below the fairway, heavily defended by sand and tall grass. JR played first. His blast was made louder by its echo bouncing among the stand of hardwoods surrounding the tee. Up the right side it thundered, missing the far bunkers but running through the fairway into the rough. His fate rested in the lie his ball had found.

King followed with a magnificent tee shot, much bolder, challenging the inside bunker and easily sailing to the fairway beyond. JR and the old man left the tee at the instant King's ball was struck and their quick steps put them a good 15 yards ahead as they charged down the fairway to assess their position.

It took the marshals in the area several minutes to find JR's ball.

The lie was *terrible*, deep in the long, twisted rough.

Immediately, the old pro voiced a positive plan. "Chop it out as best you can, somewhere short of the green. We'll get 'er up and in from there, JR, I *guarantee* it. Let's get a four here."

JR agreed. There was no possible way to advance this ball to the green. His target would have to be somewhere short of the green, preferably in the fairway. From there, he had no doubt, his short game and this wonderful old partner would take over. He just hoped he could get enough of the ball to do it.

King waited and watched. He had walked over briefly during the search and knew JR was in deep trouble. Surely, *now* he would finally put this young man away.

JR addressed his ball, firming his grip while relaxing his body. His long, velvet swing turned fierce at the bottom, trying with all its might to wrench the ball loose and into flight.

"Click..." they both heard at once. The club had made clean contact, but the long grass had nearly twisted the club from JR's hands. The ball was sailing, far to the left, past the fairway and into the bunker, well short of the green. He would now be challenged by one of golf's most difficult shots, one from a long bunker to a hole location deep in the right side of the severely sloping green, several yards distant.

King was now flush with anticipation. Without question, a great effort here would secure the Open and finally put an end to the jangling nerves of the past hour and a half. He stepped up to his shot.

The only sounds were those of a few uninterested birds, a squirrel chattering nearby, and the low rumble of a distant jet scribing its white trail in the azure sky. King was at the center of golf's universe for those seconds. His solid seven-iron never left the flagstick, boldly blazing its way to within four feet, just left of the hole. The gallery could not contain itself at the heart-pounding change of events, the seesawing of emotions that marked this duel's ebb and flow.

The old man spoke firmly to JR, demanding that he pay no attention to King's phenomenal shot, or the consequences it seemed to portend.

"Stay in the present, JR. Keep your mind on the shot at hand. All anybody can ever ask of himself is to do the absolute best with what he's been given. Come on, *we* can do this," he coached.

JR had already begun remembering where he learned the secret of executing long bunker shots like this one. It was at Q-school, a few years ago. Not *his* Q-school. The one at World Woods. King himself had made a magnificent play from a similar fairway bunker from about this distance. He had chosen a nine-iron, and later relayed to JR that the shot was nothing more than a *greenside* bunker shot with a longer club in his hands.

JR reached for the nine-iron. The old man stepped back with the bag, nodding in approval. 'I'll be damned,' he thought to himself. 'He *is* the total package.'

The world of golf had already been treated to an array of stunning and brilliant shot making from both JR and Adam King. Many of those watching in person and on national television could barely stand the tension, a tension that would only build.

JR confidently stepped into the bunker. He already knew the shot he wanted to play. He simply wanted his mind and his muscles to relax and become one with their purpose. He finally twisted his feet deep into the sand, stance open, ball forward, hands ahead. All he could see in focus was the flagstick. All else was a sea of matted color. His swing was slow and fluid, nothing was hurried, nothing rushed. The ball exploded in a giant splash of sand, flying high toward the pin 40-odd yards away.

It was all happening slowly, everything neatly packed into The Zone. The ball landed not far from King's coin. The gallery screamed. It then skipped above the hole and began spinning in place. Finally, on its last revolution, it released slowly down the slope to rising, hysterical cheers. Then, kissing the flagstick like a teenager on his first date, JR's ball *dropped out of sight.*

The gallery exploded to a level yet unreached; their roar became a shock wave of energy bounding across the course. King was stunned. JR had returned the irony of the fifth hole. King's own turn of events *there* now seemed so very long ago.

JR trotted up the slope to retrieve his ball, looking skyward and smiling broadly. He avoided King's stare of disgust.

Returning to the old man's side at the edge of the green, he held his cap aloft, acknowledging their massive approval. Bedlam rained down all around them.

The old pro lightly patted JR on the back, choking back tears, and trying to swallow the lump in his throat.

"Man, you landed a beauty on him this time. That's the greatest shot I've ever seen. Way to go, JR, *way to go.*" He was shaking. So was JR, desperately trying to catch his breath.

King knew his four-footer would still leave him one stroke ahead, but this putt was treacherous, downhill and breaking hard to the right. Not the favorite of any pro golfer, at any time. He took a deep breath and rehearsed his stroke. Two, three times. Now he was ready.

The ball started dead on line and broke quickly. It caught the lower lip, did a dramatic loop and sat motionless on the opposite edge of the hole. The gallery exploded again, but this time in total disbelief. Their running and scrambling began anew.

The once commanding lead had evaporated.

FORTY-THREE

Adrenalin is a powerful drug. A full dose now raced through JR's veins. In his mind, he could see himself, just like a cunning jockey roaring out of the last turn and into the final stretch, separating from the field and finally pulling alongside the leader and favorite. With the whip now flailing his mount's flank, he was leaning forward and screaming into the steed's upturned ear, "Now, boy, now... give me all you've got...*right now*." His heart pounded with these thoughts.

As he effortlessly climbed the hill to the eighteenth tee, the air was filled with the crackling electricity that only a super-heated gallery can produce. People were shouting his name, cheering him on and running to secure vantage points. His stunning bunker shot at the seventeenth had created a scenario most thought impossible.

JR Thompson...Adam King...dead even...one hole remaining.

His destiny now lay clearly in front of him. The U.S. Open, this extremely *personal* U.S. Open, was now at the end of JR's fingertips.

Since he could remember, he had dreamed of a moment like this, a moment that had been stolen from his father so many years ago on this very ground. Amidst all the rush and movement around him, he thought about his dad, about Billy. How he wished his father could be making this walk with him.

Approaching the tee, JR's consciousness snapped back to the moment at hand. "Stay in the present," King himself had always admonished him. In spite of the excitement, he felt surprisingly calm and his awareness of it brought a wry grin across his face.

His swing and its rhythm had been superb throughout the day and now with this scruffy old man, this wonderful new partner, at his side to guide his putting and sharpen his focus, so many of his masterful shots had already been rewarded. Could the magic last one more hole? Just a few more shots?

Surely, he thought, this one moment was what he had been born to fulfill. JR had never felt so confident, so trusting of all those lonely hours of practice, and of dreaming.

The shadows were lengthening in the late day sun, further defining the valley in front of them. The eighteenth hole at Inverness is a treacherous little par-4 of only 354 yards. The hole's major defense is at the greensite. Like all great short holes, the best strategy is developed from the hole backwards. Every hole location on the eighteenth requires a precise approach, one that can only be played from a clean fairway lie. That, in turn, creates the challenge to hit a precisely played tee shot.

On this final day, the hole was cut in a diabolical place, in a small valley at the left rear of the green, a location nearly impossible to approach and get close. The best chance for a birdie was actually not on the green at all, but from the left fringe, pin high, leaving an uphill, makeable birdie putt. Getting there would be very difficult.

JR knew all of this. He also had the honor. He could risk hitting a driver and getting closer to the green, or lay up with a fairway metal, insuring a better chance of finding the short grass. He chose the latter, knowing also that he could better control the spin of his approach from a slightly longer distance. Such a play might also put added pressure on Adam King's tee shot. JR certainly owned the moment.

One last look at his target, the distant fairway bunker on the left side of the landing area, one last exhale. The calming Zone controlled JR's brain, as if he were merely a spectator effortlessly setting the club in motion. His focus, tunnel-like, saw only the back of the ball and that distant target. All else was silent, and a blur.

The ball left the center of the clubface like a bullet, its soaring arc splitting the chosen line. Halfway through its flight, the soft fade that JR envisioned drifted the ball toward the center of the fairway. The gallery could not control its excitement as the ball came to rest scarcely 100 yards from the green. Considering the tension, it was majestic.

King, emotionless on the outside, felt slightly shaken inside. This young, untested pro, his one-time caddy and student, should have cracked long ago, but now it was he, the tour's greatest player, who was trying to hold off an incredible onslaught. It was he who was feeling the heat, instead of being the one usually applying it. King, as he had done all day, refused to back off. He chose the driver. After all, his aggressive play had produced birdies here the first two days.

King took very little time. Set up, one look, and go. Even before the gallery had completely quieted, his powerful swing produced another rocket, straight down the left side of the fairway. He casually leaned down to pick up his tee amidst polite applause and began his quick walk from the teeing grounds.

JR and the old pro were already off the tee. The gallery, too, was on the move, a huge rolling mass throwing off a variety of anonymous voices yelling out encouragement to JR.

King's ball landed well inside the fairway and within 50 yards of the green. But, as it rolled out, it came to rest in a sand-filled divot, unlucky and surely compounding the difficulty of his short approach. Something he would not know for several minutes.

By now, virtually every person on the property—fans, officials, and even several players who waited to witness the finish—were all crammed into every square inch of this tiny valley, its hillsides and giant grandstands. The entire area seemed to vibrate with excitement. The atmosphere was electric.

Anne and I had finally made our way to the elevated veranda behind the clubhouse. It overlooked the eighteenth green and was the ideal place for us to watch the final action. Our nerves had never been so jangled. Her left hand remained tightly locked in my right.

JR's ball was sitting in a perfect lie, only 102 yards from the hole. Over the green just beyond the pin was "dead," a deep little pot bunker awaited a carelessly played second. Considering the rolling contour of the green, well short was no good either. It would leave a putt nearly impossible to get down in two.

JR had the perfect shot in mind. A three-quarter pitching wedge, low flying, sent into the right side of the green. A couple of hops before the spin took over would bring the ball to the top of the ridge and hopefully, begin a slow leftward roll down the slope to the hole. He could see it as if video were already running in his mind.

He made eye contact with the old pro. The old man smiled, knowing instinctively what the young man was thinking.

Following a few practice swings and focusing on a spot wide right of the pin, JR addressed the ball. Over thirty thousand people held their collective breath in anticipation.

The shot that followed was as precise as any JR had ever played. It landed just short of the slope on the right side of the green, just as he had envisioned. Now the two hops to the top of the ridge...*perfect.*

But wait.

Instead of stopping and rolling slowly sideways down the slope to the hole, on the second bounce the ball jolted backwards. It had just a little too much spin...and now his ball was rolling helplessly back toward the front of the green.

The shrieks and moans from the gallery were palpable. JR's heart sank. The old pro's shoulders slumped. The shot that had been *so close* to greatness now limped over and handed momentum to King. Surely now, he would finally seize the moment.

The gallery was again unsettled as King began looking over his shot. He knew that a full shot from a sand-filled divot was not that difficult for a world-class player like himself.

"Play it back in your stance and hit the ball on the downswing," he said softly to himself, "just like all other fairway shots."

But this one was different. It was not really a full shot because he had driven the ball so close to the green. And, of course, this was the last hole of the U.S. Open.

King decided to play it like a long bunker shot. That way he could be very aggressive, using the sand to cushion the blow. At the worst, he would come up a little short of the cup and considering JR's nearly impossible position, a par for King was likely to win the Open right here. The thought process was clear, the plan solid. He had hit this shot hundreds of times in practice and numerous times during his race to the top of the PGA Tour's money list. Simple. Stay down and trust it.

To everyone watching, the shot King played was amazing, a soft, high floating shot flown all the way to the hole. But King knew immediately that the divot was deeper than he had thought, that there had been more sand under his ball than he had imagined. It would not have the spin he had originally counted on.

The ball landed inches from the hole, eliciting a tremendous roar, but the harsh first bounce that King knew was coming carried it to the back fringe, where it hesitated and then began trickling slowly down the slope. On its last roll, it fell into the treacherous little pot bunker.

Now, each of them was in serious trouble. Even with King off the green, he was still much closer to the hole. JR would play first.

JR and King walked onto the green to thunderous applause. The gallery was showing their appreciation for the mind-boggling battle that they had waged. No one had ever seen anything like it. Everyone knew JR's story, and the vast majority were openly pulling for him. However, their tribute was also for the popular Adam King who had played inspired and aggressive golf in the face of JR's brilliant charge.

JR marked his ball before they finished their applause, took a quick look at the difficulty facing him and tossed the ball gently to the old pro. He then took a few seconds to scan the entire scene, this phenomenal cathedral in this beautiful little valley. Everywhere he looked, thousands of eyes were drinking in the moment. Somehow, he sensed his father was with him. He could feel him. Win or lose, he knew Billy would have been immensely proud of his son. He also wondered if his dad was watching, somewhere, alongside his grandfather. Somehow, he could feel that they had, at last, become friends. An ironic time, he smiled to himself, for thoughts like those.

The old pro had already begun stalking the incredibly difficult task they had before them. He knew the putt would be virtually impossible to stop near the cup. Struck too lightly and the ball would stay on top of the ridge, a shade too hard and it would race down the hill past the hole and into the rough at the edge of the green. The straight line from ball to hole measured 62 feet, but this widely curving putt would traverse a much longer route than that.

Doc walked JR up the slope to a spot nearly 20 feet to the right of the hole.

"This is a two-part putt, JR."

He pointed to an old ball mark just at the crest of the slope. JR looked into the old man's eyes. They were clear, resolute, and certain.

"To have *any* chance at all, our ball will have to begin its roll down the slope to the hole from this *very* spot."

The first part of the plan would require that JR putt his ball nearly 60 feet up the slope and virtually stop it on *this one little spot,* the size of a dime. The second part, the old pro said matter-of-factly, "was up to God." But they both knew it was their only chance.

Finally, the old pro, eyes glistening and throat swelling, turned to JR and said, "Today, for me, has been the treasure of a lifetime." He paused to gain some composure. "Trust yourself, son."

JR looked into his eyes once again. What he saw, glowing back at him, was an overflowing pride, evidence that the old man had indeed treasured their experience.

'There is an awful lot to this old man,' he thought. 'Thank God he stepped into my path.'

JR surveyed the all-important first leg of the monster he faced, taking practice swings with his putter, never taking his eye off the spot, simply letting his eyes and his brain compute the perfect speed. His vision never included the pin now being held intently by the old pro. Then, just as at the tee, a wonderful calm came over JR as he addressed the ball. The Zone still held him.

Everything was in slow motion again, his shoulders smoothly rocked back and through and with no conscious effort on his part, the putt was away, running hot up the slope, to the right of the spot. Up the slope it climbed, slowing and turning left. JR's eyes began widening, the gallery's vocal anticipation rising, as the ball slowly approached the spot. Slowing...slowing...until it reached the spot...and *stopped*.

JR was now charging up the slope, demanding, ordering the ball to move. He was halfway up the slope when it happened. The second or so that it took seemed like an eternity. The ball wobbled at first, then moved imperceptibly from one dimple to the next, and then the next. The individual little wiggles turned into a trickle, then a slow roll, picking up speed and began racing, torpedo-like, toward the hole below.

By now, JR had reached the top of the slope, fist pumping, his thunderous voice lost among thousands. The old pro's eyes flared as he watched it come, his heart pounded like never before. Flagstick now removed and held high above his head,

he was joined by the throng's crescendo, everyone together, hysterically willing the ball down the slope. Then...*staccato!* possibly the *single loudest roar* anyone in golf could ever remember.

With its line dead true, the ball slammed into the back of the cup, popped into the air and slipped into the sweet darkness of history.

JR could barely breathe. His feet never touched the ground. The gallery strained at the ropes, jumping and shrieking wildly, taking several minutes to settle. King stood in total shock. JR's final lightning bolt had gone right through him.

He tried to gather himself by taking extra time to prepare, but his bunker shot never threatened the hole. Joyous bedlam broke out all over again. JR turned to hug the old pro. His golf bag and the flagstick now lay alone at the edge of the green.

The old man was *gone.*

The sun broke between two fluffy clouds, sending fresh, warm beams to bathe the scene. The old pro had simply vanished.

Above the din of wild gallery noise, JR heard the triumphant, sweet chorus of a thousand bugles, more beautiful than anything he had ever heard.

Surrounded by the pandemonium, he momentarily closed his eyes. His lifelong dream had just come true, its mission accomplished. Engulfed by the sound of those glorious bugles, JR could feel his father's arms wrapped tightly around him. It was a comfort he relished, one that reached deep into his childhood memories.

A voice began calling in his mind, a whisper at first, barely audible, then growing in volume, "thank you, cowboy," it said. Then again, clear as crystal, "Thank you, my little cowboy…for everything," came the voice of the *old pro*.

Quietly, inside the ancient clubhouse of Inverness, an old, fervent wish was being granted, a Divine promise fulfilled.

A silversmith was engraving the latest name on the U.S. Open trophy.

It was the name that JR had requested.

It was the name…of *Billy Thompson*.